GW00492672

Death at the Manor

An Asharton Manor Mystery: Book 1

Celina Grace

© Celina Grace 2014

Death at the Manor
Copyright © 2014 by Celina Grace. All rights reserved.
First Print Edition: 2015

No part of this book may be reproduced, scanned, or distributed in any printed or electronic form without permission. Please do not participate in or encourage piracy of copyrighted materials in violation of the author's rights. Thank you for respecting the hard work of this author.

This is a work of fiction. Names, characters, places, and incidents either are the product of the author's imagination or are used fictitiously, and any resemblance to locales, events, business establishments, or actual persons—living or dead—is entirely coincidental.

This book is for my brother, Anthony, with love.

I'd never seen anything like that house before in my life. Even using the word 'house' doesn't sound right; it doesn't convey the impression I want. I started off as a kitchen maid in one of the townhouses in Brighton and I'd thought they were grand enough, but they look like the meanest, dingiest old hovels compared to Asharton Manor. It was like Buckingham Palace, I'm telling you; the grandest place I'd ever set eyes on or foot in. They'd sent a car to meet me at the station. It was only about the third time I'd ever been in a car, and I was still recovering from the novelty when I had the shock of seeing the manor for the first time. As the car rattled up the driveway, I looked out of the window and I could feel my eyes becoming rounder and my mouth doing the same. It was four stories of golden stone, the drive sweeping around the front of it; a fountain shot upwards before it, so that the front door could only be seen through a mist of silver droplets. The front seemed to have hundreds of windows and they all glittered in the sun. They gave the place a blank, closed-in look. Although impressive, it wasn't a welcoming house.

We drove on past the front door, of course, round

the back to the stables and the servants' quarters. The driver hadn't said one word to me, apart from addressing me at the station: *"Car for Miss Joan Hart, that you?"* Perhaps he was a bit put out to have been sent for someone so lowly. It was a step up for me, getting this job here, head kitchen maid, but unless you're the butler or the housekeeper, you're never going to get much respect from the rest of the servants. I didn't let it bother me. I was still too astonished that I was going to be living here, in a house like something you might see in films. Asharton Manor. It was a queer name. It didn't seem to belong to the village, which was called Midford, about twenty miles west from Chippenham. I hadn't been to this part of the country before – all my places beforehand had been in cities and my previous position had been in London. I wondered what it would be like, living in the country.

I wasn't able to wonder much further as, by that time, I was in the kitchen, trying not to wilt before the stares of the other kitchen staff. It was a big, low-ceilinged place, with stone flags on the floor and the biggest kitchen range I'd ever seen on one side. I sighed inwardly as I thought about how long it would take to black-lead, but then brightened a little when I realised that it probably wouldn't be my job anymore. Here, I hoped I would learn some proper cooking.

The cook came over and introduced herself to

me as Mrs. Cotting. In all the places I've worked, the cooks have either been thin or stout. It's funny, but there never seemed to be any cook that was in the middle, size-wise. The thin ones had given up on eating – cooking does that sometimes, it robs you of your appetite – and the fat ones had sampled too many of their own dishes. Mrs. Cotting was a thin cook and she had a sharp, shrewish kind of face that I didn't much like. But, I must say, she shook hands quite cordially, although her glance at me was frankly assessing.

"You look strong enough, gel," was her opening remark and I nodded. I am strong, I've been a woman's size and shape since I was eleven years old and my 'heftiness' was what won me the first job I ever had. It was a shame that my face was so homely, not that a skivvie's uniform was ever very flattering. You weren't supposed to have a bit of hair showing under your cap and mine is the sort of face that could do with a bit of framing.

"You're in at the deep end, tonight," Mrs. Cotting said brusquely. "We've got a welcome back dinner for the mistress's brother, so that's eighteen sitting down to table."

I quailed a little inwardly but managed to nod firmly, as if that were going to be no bother at all.

"You'll want to see your room," said the housekeeper, Mrs. Smith. I'd met her once before, at my interview. She was a big but graceful woman, with a no-nonsense Irish brogue. "You'll be sharing with Annie, the under housemaid."

She beckoned to Annie, who was a shy looking girl with smooth brown hair. She looked nice enough and I was glad.

"Take Joan to her room, Annie, and get her settled. Joan, Mrs. Cotting will want you back down here in half an hour. Do you know how to set up a table?"

"Yes, of course," I said, slightly snappishly. I mean, honestly. That was one of the first things I learned on the job. Mrs. Smith frowned a little and I dropped my eyes, chastised, and bobbed an apologetic little curtsey. I didn't want to start off on the wrong foot straight away.

Annie and I climbed the back stairs to our room, which was one of the small ones located up in under the eaves. Later, I was able to climb the main staircase, which was very grand, but the servants' staircase was shabby and didn't even have carpet, just scuffed linoleum.

We climbed the stairs for what seemed like hours. Luckily my trunk wasn't heavy – it wasn't as if I owned a lot of things.

"You're from London, aren't you?" Annie asked, shyly.

"Yes."

"Do you get to see the films much there?"

I blinked. "Um... sometimes."

"I love the talkies," said Annie. "We don't have a theatre anywhere near here, worst luck. Bristol's the nearest and that's such a long way away it takes up all your day off. Must be lovely to live in London."

"Well," I said, a little helplessly. "I suppose so."

"Ramón Novarro's my favourite," said Annie. "Who's yours?"

"Um..." I said again, but was saved from replying by the fact that we'd finally reached the top of the stairs. Puffing, we both came out into a dark little corridor, with several doors leading off it. The ceiling was low enough for me to cringe a little and duck my head.

"Down here," said Annie and led me through the last door along the corridor. Our room was a typical one; whitewashed walls, no paint or wallpaper here. Iron bedsteads along the wall, each with a lumpy mattress made up with the cast-off bedding of the better portions of the house. A washstand stood on a little wooden table between the beds and a small, battered looking wardrobe leaned against the wall. I could tell which bed was Annie's – the wall beside it was plastered with pictures of Novarro and other movie stars, obviously torn out of various film magazines. It made me smile a little inside.

I was never much one for the talkies; I preferred the music halls. My friend Verity and I used to go as often as we could afford it. Verity's family had had connections with the theatre and sometimes we

would be able to get free tickets and even get to go
backstage to meet the performers. That was a real
thrill. I felt a surge of loneliness when I realised
Verity was now hundreds of miles away. I made up
my mind to write to her as soon as I got a moment
to myself.

Annie cast herself onto her bed, which creaked
like a ship in a gale. I knew mine would be the
same. I heaved my trunk onto the bedspread – yes,
a jangle of springs like a pair of clashing cymbals –
and began to unpack.

"We've got someone almost as good as a film star
here at the moment," said Annie after a moment,
giggling. "Madam's brother. You should see him,
he's so good looking."

"Oh yes?" I said, trying to sound interested.

"He only came back from Africa about two weeks
ago." She pronounced 'Africa' in an awed tone. "He's
been living out there for years. You should see how
brown he is. Brown as a berry!"

That phase has always struck me as rather
foolish. I can't think of any berries that are actually
brown. I smiled politely and then thought, well, at
least I can find out a bit more about the people I'm
going to work for.

"What's the mistress like?" I asked, genuinely
curious.

Annie pulled a face. "She's a pain. Always
moaning about her health and wanting different

things and then not wanting them when she gets them."

"Is she unwell, then?"

Annie rolled her eyes. "Thinks she is. Always taking to her bed for one thing or another."

My heart sank. That meant a lot of cooking different dishes to try and 'tempt an invalid's palate'. Still, Mrs. Cotting had no doubt been here a while, she probably had Madam well managed. I hoped so.

Annie chatted on. "Then there's Miss Cleo, the mistress's best friend. She's staying here for the summer. Very glamorous, she is, looks just like Louise Brooks. She's an Honourable." She stumbled a little over the syllables. I tried to look impressed.

"And the master?"

"He's all right. Quiet. Mostly he's up in London during the week. His aunt lives here too - she's a fussy old thing, always messing about with flowers. Mrs. Carter-Knox. Her and Madam don't get on too well."

"In what way?"

Annie giggled. "Mrs. Carter-Knox is always doing these big flower arrangements and Madam doesn't like them. Calls them 'vulgar'. I can't see anything wrong with them, to be honest. I suppose they're a bit big."

I nodded. Flower arranging... I wanted to roll my eyes. Who had time to mess about with sticking flowers in a vase but a woman who had nothing else to do?

I DIDN'T ACTUALLY SEE THE mistress until she came down to the kitchen, two days later, to discuss menus with Mrs. Cotting. She was pretty, I'll give her that; little and blonde and dainty, with her hair in lovely marcelled waves over her shapely head. She wore diamond earrings, so whenever she turned her head there was an answering sparkle that flashed from her ears. She was quite simply dressed, but you could tell that whatever she was wearing cost the absolute earth.

I stood respectfully by while she and Mrs. Cotting talked. I've worked in households where the cooking was on the plain side and I've worked in Jewish houses, where they had all sorts of outlandish dishes, but I realised, after listening to Madam, that here I would be cooking the fanciest, most messed-about, fashionable dishes you could have. I didn't mind that, so much – it was always interesting to try something new and I've always liked a challenge. What I could have done without was Madam's simpering little voice; a soft, flannelly sort of voice that, I was sure, could easily become shrewish.

Still, she wasn't as such talking to me. She wafted

out of the door after about twenty minutes and Mrs. Cotting beckoned me over.

"You can make a start on this sauce, Joan," she said. "You'll find everything you need in the larder and the cool box."

They didn't scrimp on the food at Asharton Manor, I'll give them that. Every day we had deliveries of fresh meat, milk, cream and cheese and the fish man came around three times a week. That first night I was there we'd done six courses, starting with a savoury, a soup, a fish course, the main course—which was rack of lamb—followed by pudding, then cheese, fruit and coffee. It being my first day on the job and all that, what with the travelling I'd done and the worry of all the new faces and ways, it was a miracle I didn't drop dead with exhaustion. But, as I've said before, I'm young and strong and managed to somehow get through it. Luckily that was the only entertaining they did that week; although as I worked there, I grew to realise that they liked to entertain a lot.

I didn't see the mistress or the master, the brother or anyone else the day after the dinner party. Sleeping off all the wine and cocktails and brandy they'd consumed, no doubt. Mrs. Cotting had gone to bed at midnight but I'd had to stay up 'til one o'clock to get the kitchen shipshape. Annie was a vague snoring shape in the other bed by the time I'd stumbled up the stairs to our room. I didn't even wash, I was so tired; I just stripped off my clothes and rolled into bed. One thing hard work does for you, it gives you a good sleep. I didn't stir until Annie woke me at six thirty the next morning and, even though I'd barely had six hours sleep, I felt quite sprightly again and eager to make a start.

One morning after I'd been there a week, I was walking back to the kitchen door, my feet crunching over the gravel, when a man rounded the corner. I knew immediately who it was – the mistress's brother. He had a shotgun slung over one shoulder and an old felt hat pushed back on his head. I saw what Annie had meant. He was very good looking, fair hair greased back but with a lock that fell over one eye. You could see the resemblance to the mistress, something in the chin and the cheekbones, but he didn't have her fair skin. He looked like a polished bronze statue, he was so brown.

"Hello," he greeted me. "I don't believe we've met before."

I could feel myself flushing red as a beetroot. Why was he talking to me, when he could clearly see by my uniform that I was a servant?

"I'm John Manfield," he went on, easy as you like. "You must be Joan. Did you do those delicious little pork things at the dinner the other night?"

I managed to pull myself together and nod. After a moment, I came to my senses and curtseyed.

"Oh, don't bother about that," Mr. Manfield said,

hefting his rifle onto the other broad shoulder. "Can't stand the stuffiness of this country, sometimes. Not like this in Africa. Well, I'd better get on."

He tipped his felt hat to me – I felt my cheeks go scarlet once more – and sauntered off. I was so flustered I found myself walking into the dairy rather than the kitchen and had to turn myself about and retrace my steps.

"Oh, he's always like that," Mrs. Cotting said a little later, when I had to explain why I'd messed up the mayonnaise. I was still a bit flustered at being talked to as a, well, an ordinary person, by a member of the gentry.

"He's used to native servants," Mrs. Cotting went on. "He's always talking to us if he comes across us. Makes the mistress mad but he just shrugs it off."

"He's got an eye for the girls, too," said Meg, the little kitchen maid, with a giggle.

"That will do, Margaret," said Mrs. Cotting sharply. "Don't be forgetting your place, now."

"Sorry," Meg said, abashed. We bent to our work again but, after a moment, I caught her eye and winked, and she stifled another giggle.

Miss Cleo was dark as the mistress was fair, with a clever face and a very drawling, sardonic voice, a complete contrast to Madam. She came down with her to the kitchen one day, dressed in her cream satin house-pyjamas, if you please, and wafted about, sticking her face into the larder and lifting up lids on the saucepans on the Rayburn, bold as brass. All the while, she smoked a cigarette in a long, ebony holder. I thought Mrs. Cotting was going to have a fit. It would have been funny, if I hadn't known I'd be the one to have to deal with the aftermath. Of course, Mrs. Cotting would never have said anything to Cleo Maddox's face – she had a *title*, after all. Instead, Mrs. Cotting would vent her anger on Meg and me.

I quite often saw Miss Cleo in the garden; swimming in the pool, playing tennis with Mr. Manfield or sometimes Mr. Denford. Annie told me, in a scandalised tone, that she had been seen down at the river one dawn morning, swimming with *nothing on*. She was the talk of the village, apparently, but it didn't seem to bother her. The rich are like that, though; things that would bury someone of the working class merely slid off them like oil. She seemed a bit of an odd friend for the mistress to have, to be honest. They were so different, both in looks and in manner, but again, perhaps it's different for those with money. They like to be with people like themselves.

The master himself was very different to both his wife and her brother. He was a stockbroker, whatever that was, and he was a thin, short man with very black hair and a neatly trimmed moustache. According to Violet, the lady's maid, he was soft-spoken, gentlemanlike in his manners, and quiet.

"He's always struck me as a bit lonely," she said one evening, when we were talking in the servants' hall. "Doesn't seem to talk to the mistress much, or she doesn't talk to him. Been even more like that since her brother came back and now Miss Cleo is here."

"Wasn't that how they met?" said Annie. She was smoking a cigarette which she'd cadged from Albert, one of the stable boys, and I was trying not to cough.

Violet nodded. "Mister John introduced them, out on his ranch in Africa. The master was a friend of his, Mister John's."

"I'd like to go to Africa," I said, not really thinking.

Violet snorted. "Catch you saving up enough to go to Africa," she said, laughing. "Honestly, Joan."

I smiled dutifully at my supposed silliness, but I was aware of a spurt of anger. Why shouldn't I go to Africa? Wasn't I allowed to dream? The trouble with Violet, and with all the girls I knew except for Verity, is that their dreams were so small. All they wanted from life was marriage, to a tradesman or the under-footman; marriage and babies and perhaps two rooms to call their own. I wanted more than that. Surely there was more to life than that? And what man would ever marry me anyway, with my plain face and my towering frame? No, I knew that life wouldn't hold much romance for me. That was why I was trying to learn to cook, so I would always be able to support myself.

Verity was the same. She may have been only a housemaid (although at Lord Carthright's place, so not exactly a two-a-penny establishment), but she knew what it was like to have to take care of yourself from an early age. We'd met in the orphanage when I was ten and she was eleven. Our beds had been next to one another in the dormitory and we'd whisper after the lights went out, about all the amazing things we were going to do when we were grown up. Dreams were all we had in the orphanage, they were what sustained us.

As luck would have it, the post brought a letter from Verity that day. I read it up in my room after the day's work, by the light of the flickering candle set in the holder on my bedside table. I was so tired my eyes kept closing, but I forced them open again and again. I chuckled at Verity's descriptions of how the butler in her household had got so drunk on the dregs of champagne from one of Lord Carthright's parties that he'd fallen down the last two stairs to the scullery. Verity and Mrs. Antells, the housekeeper, had had to *roll* him along the corridor to his room as he was too heavy for them to lift and had to leave him propped up against his bed, snoring drunkenly. He *was* an old sot, I remembered, having met him once when I'd been there for tea.

Verity signed off her letter with "Joanie, you

must write to me again soon, I love receiving your letters. Your descriptions of Asharton Manor are so vivid I feel like I'm there with you. Tell me more about living in the country and whether you're learning any new dishes, and if the mistress is still having the vapours all over the place. And come to London when you can, I miss you."

I smiled as I folded up the letter and put it in my bedside table. It might be slightly immodest of me to say, but I do have a good way with words. I find it easy to put them together in pleasing sentences. At least, I think they're pleasing. Verity's not the only person to have told me I write good letters. It was knowledge I hugged close to myself, when the days in the kitchen seemed so long, and the work so hard, and I didn't seem to be getting any better at cookery. At least writing was something I could do well.

Verity's last paragraph recurred to me the next morning. The mistress had come down to go through the menus with Mrs. Cotting and, having not seen her for a week or so, I was somewhat shocked at her appearance. I'd rather mockingly described her 'illnesses' to Verity as the bored fancies of an idle woman, but today she looked properly unwell; pale and thin and with her golden hair dulled somehow, as if the shine had worn off it. She talked to Mrs. Cotting in a listless tone, as if food were the last thing she was thinking about.

Perhaps she was in the family way, at long last, for all she'd lost weight. It can take some women like that, at first. She'd had some sickness, as we heard from Violet in great, and in my opinion unnecessary, detail when she came down to sit with us in the servants' hall, that evening. I was trying to read a book but had to shut the covers in the end, as Violet went on and on about the mistress's illness and how she moped around her room all day and had a row with the master.

"Fighting like cats and dogs, they were," said Violet with relish. "She was crying and he stormed off. Wouldn't surprise me if she's up the spout and it's not his, you know."

"Violet!" I said, genuinely shocked. Mrs. Cotting was in her own sitting room, or you can be sure Violet would never have said such a thing. "How can you say that?"

Violet looked sly. "I see things, you know," she said. "He's not been in her bed in weeks. And she's fainting and crying and sick all the time. Can't be anything else, can it?"

I could feel myself blushing. "Well, you might be right, but it's not for us to speculate, is it?" I said and opened my book again. Violet snorted – she had a most unattractive way of doing that – and she and little Meg went outside to smoke a cigarette and gossip some more.

Nothing more was said about the mistress and,

in a week or so, she got well again and began to look better. She didn't appear to get any stouter, so that theory of Violet's was complete nonsense, in my opinion. I overheard her and Miss Cleo laughing about Mrs. Carter-Knox's latest monstrous flower arrangement which stood in the hallway, looming like a piece of jungle stuck in a large vase.

"Darling, one expects to see a team of explorers emerging, with pith helmets," Miss Cleo drawled, and Madam giggled. I felt a bit sorry for Mrs. Carter-Knox. She always struck me as the odd one out, a middle-aged lady in a house full of young people. Her husband had been the master's uncle and he'd died fairly young, leaving her a childless widow at forty-eight. Apparently, she'd come for a visit last year and just stayed on, which was another source of friction between the Denfords, according to the gossipy Violet.

I'd been hoping to go to London on my next day off, and had been saving up for the ticket. But, as it happened, Verity and I weren't able to coordinate our days off in order to be able to meet. I was disappointed, but tried to console myself with the thought that we'd manage it soon. There was so much I wanted to tell her that wasn't always something I could put in a letter. Like the time I went for a walk in the woods around the manor.

That was a very queer thing. The more I've thought about it, the stranger it seems. It was my afternoon off and it was such a lovely day I thought I'd spend it exploring a bit more of the grounds. There were apparently some lovely walks in the woods that surrounded the estate and, although I was slightly nervous about getting lost, I decided to go for a bit of a tramp about. I packed up some sandwiches and a flask of tea and set off. I passed Mrs. Carter-Knox in the garden, cutting flowers for another of her arrangements, while Miss Cleo and the mistress drank cocktails in the conservatory. I sighed for a moment at the unfairness of life. What I wouldn't give to be able to swan around, poking flowers into vases and then retiring back to my rooms, exhausted, for a nap, just as Mrs. Carter-Knox did every day. What I wouldn't give to sit in a luxurious conservatory and swig cocktails, lifting the glass with my fingers covered in diamond rings, knowing I could sit there all day if I wanted to, because I didn't have to cook, or wash up, or scrub down the kitchen table. Why hadn't I been born into a highborn family? Why did I have to be poor and work for my living?

I stomped out of the gardens and followed the footpath to the woods, feeling cross at the unfairness of life. After a few moments, though, I began to cheer up. It was a sunny day, with the blue sky covered in scudding white clouds – warm for May. I had to be back by six and I wasn't planning on being out longer than a couple of hours. I really didn't want to have to find my way back through the woods in the dark.

I walked, at first keeping the manor in sight but, as I grew more confident, I struck out on the smaller paths that wound through the beech trees. They were majestic trees and walking down a line of them felt almost as though I were walking through somewhere like a cathedral. The old brown leaves rustled beneath my feet as I walked and the woods were alive with bird song. I was enjoying myself so much I barely noticed that I was straying farther and farther into the woods. The trees gradually began to change, from the smooth-skinned beeches, to the gnarled oaks and the darker evergreens. They grew ever more thickly about the path and my steps began to be more and more hesitant.

Eventually, I stopped. I was in some sort of vague clearing, in the midst of a thick forest of pines. The sun had gone behind a cloud and the noises of the forest somehow became muted and then stilled altogether. I stood uncertainly, looking about me. The clearing was about forty foot wide and in the middle stood a jumble of stone. I walked a little closer. As I got closer, I could see that the stone was actually broken masonry. Had a house once stood here? I looked about me, at the forest pressing in on all sides. Suddenly, I felt swamped by a wave of uneasiness. No, it was stronger than that. It was fear.

I turned, my hand up to my throat, heart thudding. The silence pressed down on me like a thick blanket and my ears buzzed. Then, above the noise of my heartbeat, I heard a distinct sound – a loud crack as a twig snapped underfoot. My fear leapt up another notch. Was there someone following me? Chasing me? I am ashamed to say I was almost panting, my heart racing. I saw a figure through the dark branches of the trees, moving towards me, and nearly screamed. Then, as he stepped out into the clearing, a surge of relief made my knees weaken. It was John Manfield, the mistress's brother.

He walked up to me, his gun crooked over his arm, smiling and whistling. All of a sudden, my panic seemed incomprehensible. The smile I gave him in return was possibly far too eager, but I was just so relieved to see a familiar face.

"Good afternoon," he said. "Out for a walk?"

Now that I had myself under control again, I was beginning to feel uncomfortable in a different way. I simply could not stand and chat to this man in a manner in which I could have chatted to a man of my own class. The knowledge of the gulf between us closed up my throat and I could only nod, dumbly.

"Certainly a lovely day for it," said Mr. Manfield. He looked at me a little more closely. "Are you quite well, Joan?"

The terror of the past few minutes must still have shown in my face. Impulsively, I said, "I was afraid I was lost. I found this clearing and – well, it was strange..."

I trailed off. I didn't even really know what I was trying to say. But Mr. Manfield was looking at me as if he understood.

"Gave you a bit of a turn, did it?" he asked, and I found myself nodding. "Yes, it's a strange place. Used to be an old place of worship here, you know. A long time ago."

"Really?" I was interested, despite myself.

Mr. Manfield nodded, staring about him at the encircling trees. "The vicar was telling me about it, last Sunday. They used to worship one of the heathen goddesses here. Astarte, she was called. Pretty strange stuff used to go on here, by all accounts."

I could feel myself blushing. Heathen goddesses sounded like the sort of topic where some men would take the opportunity to make some rather broad jokes. As that occurred to me, it also occurred to me that I was alone in the middle of a wood with a man, a man who apparently had 'an eye for the girls'. What if he—? I wondered what would be worse, to run or to stay...

I've worked in a few places where the masters were awful. One place was so bad for it that you were afraid to even go to the privy on your own, in case you were grabbed. I didn't last long, there. But, I had to say, I didn't get the sort of feeling from Mr.

Manfield. He didn't seem like he would be a threat in that way – I don't know how I could have felt that, but I did. I relaxed a little but kept myself wary.

We both stood looking at the trees. They looked oddly as though they were watching us back and I couldn't suppress a shiver.

Mr. Manfield glanced at me. "The villagers still won't come here," he said. "Not if they don't have to. I suppose every village has its memories. Bad ones."

I nodded, although I wasn't exactly sure of what he was saying.

"Human sacrifice," he said softly. I could feel my eyebrows shoot up and I began to feel nervous again. Mr. Manfield went on. "Astarte, the goddess – apparently they used to make sacrifices to her, here. Mostly animals but a few people, now and again. Horrible business, what?"

I nodded again, fervently.

"That's where the manor gets its name," he went on. "It's a corruption of Astarte."

"I wondered where it came from. It's a queer name."

"Yes, it is. The whole set-up is queer, isn't it?"

He was talking to me again like an equal. It made me thrilled and uneasy, in equal measure.

"Reminds me of Africa, you know," said Mr. Manfield, ruminatively. "I lived on the east coast, a place called Teganka. My local tribe had some odd superstitions. Thought they could ill-wish people. A bit rum, you know, because people did actually sicken and die, sometimes. Odd thing, superstition..."

The sun came out suddenly, dappling the clearing with golden light. I felt my heart actually lift and the odd feeling of dread and oppression suddenly lifted.

"Can you find your way back?" asked Mr Manfield. I wondered whether he'd experienced the same lightening of spirit as I had. He certainly looked a little happier.

"Oh, yes, sir. I'm quite sure I can get back. Thank you."

"Well, I'd best be off then. If you're sure...?"

"Quite sure, thank you sir. You're very kind."

"Righto." He tipped his hat to me and strode off, hoisting his gun up onto his shoulder. I watched him walk away and then turned myself and began to retrace my steps, as quickly as I could without actually running. I'd had enough of the glories of nature. I wanted to be back amongst people. Even the thought of all the hard work awaiting me, later that evening, didn't slow me down.

Things continued uneventfully for a week or so. The master went up to London, the mistress came down every day with her menus for Mrs. Cotting. I saw Mr. Manfield go off in the direction of the woods, with his gun over his shoulder, almost every morning that week. He seemed to prefer being outdoors, unlike the mistress who was rarely seen in the gardens. I wondered whether they were close. He seemed to enjoy the company of Mrs. Carter-Knox; they would often be found talking about wildlife and gardening and exotic plants. Apparently she'd spent some time in Africa too and they often spoke about their time there. Miss Cleo spent most of her time with the mistress, although I had once come across her and the master in the library, talking together in low voices. She and Mr. Manfield didn't seem to have much to do with one another. In fact, I would have said that they were downright prickly with one another, but I had no idea why. I would have liked to have a brother, or any sibling, really. Verity was the closest thing to a sister I had, and she was a blessing to be remembered if ever I felt a little down and lonely about my place in the world.

Then the mistress got ill again. This time, the doctor was called and I saw him leaving the building and driving away in his black car, very neat and correct in his suit and hat. He'd been shown to the bedroom by Mrs. Smith and she came into the kitchen shortly after that with the tray of food that Mrs. Cotting had prepared for the mistress.

"She didn't fancy it, then?" I said, looking at the array of untouched dishes on the tray.

"Oh, she's worse this time," said Mrs. Smith. "Can't keep anything down. And she has strange – fancies, I think you'd call them. Delusions." She hesitated for a moment. "I think Doctor's quite worried."

"Humph," said Mrs. Cotting. "We'll soon see her up and about again, mark my words."

Funnily enough, Mrs. Cotting was right. Two days later, the mistress was up and about again, wafting about the house in her beautiful clothes. But she looked – I don't know – strange. Almost as if she were listening to something no one else could hear. The master came back from town that night and the two of them dined alone. Mr. Manfield had gone to visit a friend and Miss Cleo was up in London for the night. Mrs. Carter-Knox had ordered a tray to be brought up to her room. She often did that, which annoyingly made for extra work. Luckily, the table menu tonight was quite simple, for a change; clear soup, a chicken and mushroom pie and then a savoury at the end instead of a sweet. Annie was ill in bed with a bad cold and so I had to wait at table, which I normally hated doing. I felt so big and clumsy in the parlour maid's uniform and I was always afraid I would drop a dish or, worse, spill something hot on one of the guests.

The dining room was silent as I moved around the table, proffering the vegetables. There was no conversation between husband and wife, no sound except for the chime of cutlery on china and the crackle and spit of the fire. Perhaps it was always like this, I had no way of knowing. As I waited for the mistress to serve herself a miniscule portion of chicken pie, I realised that I'd forgotten to bring up the gravy. Quickly I looked up to see if the butler, Mr. Pettigrew, had noticed, but he was busying himself at the drinks cabinet. As soon as I decently could, I quietly left the room and pounded down the back stairs to the kitchen.

Thankfully the gravy was still hot – Meg, bless her heart, had put it in the top of the Rayburn to keep warm. I gave her a grateful smile as I dashed back across the kitchen floor, holding the jug in front of me like a trophy. Back up the stairs, nineteen to the dozen, and my hand was on the door to the dining room when I heard the mistress's hissing voice, which cut through my own jagged breathing. She was saying something to the master in a tone so loaded with venom it stopped me in my tracks.

"You do it to torment me, I think you get pleasure out of it—"

"Oh, Delphine..." The master's voice was bored and a little annoyed. I stayed rigid for a moment, behind the door.

The mistress spoke again, her voice ragged. "Why you and John have to be at each other's throats all the time, I don't know. You're always fighting and it makes it so hard for me. You have no idea what my life is like, none at all."

"That's not the case—"

She cut across him. "If you're not having cosy

little chats with Cleo, or boring on with your aunt, you're ignoring me. I could be invisible, for all you care."

"Delphine, now that's wrong—"

She cut across him again. "I hate you," she said and the sentence ended on a sob.

I was holding my breath (which was not easy after running down and up a flight of stairs), but nearly screamed when there was a ponderous clearing of a throat behind me. I turned to see Mr. Pettigrew, with a newly opened bottle of port in his hand.

"What seems to be the problem, Joan?" he asked, frowning.

"Nothing - nothing at all," I stuttered and pushed open the dining room door with my free hand.

Madam had her golden head down, her fingers clenched around the silver cutlery. I thought I saw a tear fall onto her plate. Mr. Denford was busy cutting up his pie but his jaw was clenched – in fact, his whole body was clenched, tight, like an angry fist. I put the gravy on the table, prickling all over with embarrassment. Had they realised I'd been listening at the door? Before I could think anything else, the mistress dropped the knife and fork with a musical tinkle, pushed back her chair and fled the room. I could see Mr. Pettigrew regarding her with astonished eyes before his training took over and the mask of the impersonal servant settled back over his features.

If I had been Violet, I would have regaled the other servants with this little piece of drama. I didn't, though. It felt wrong, to have eavesdropped and to be witness to such emotional distress. What had the mistress meant? Did the master and her brother not get along? I thought of the way she'd said *cosy little chats with Cleo,* in a voice loaded with sarcastic meaning. As I got undressed that night and put my weary bones to bed, I thought of the hissed venom in her voice, clear enough even through a wooden door.

Annie was back in her position the next day, sniffling, coughing and red-eyed, but I was too thankful not to have to wait at table again to be too sorry for her. I made her a hot toddy when Mrs. Cotting's back was turned, with an extra spoonful of Madeira in it. There were no extra guests expected this week and it was with a small shock that I realised there hadn't been any real entertainment at the manor for over a month. The vicar and his wife had come to dinner a week ago, but that had been a comparatively simple menu and Mrs. Cotting, Meg and I had coped with it without really turning a hair. I thought back to the frantic days when I'd first arrived; the elaborate menus, the multitude of guests that would arrive for sumptuous banquets. Now all that had gone.

I busied myself with the mayonnaise, but I was all fingers and thumbs; it just wouldn't mix properly. Instead of a smooth, thick, creamy paste the colour of custard, all I was getting was curdled cream and separated eggs. I threw away the latest lumpy batch and began again, slowly dripping in the olive oil, one bit at a time, and whisking it steadily. I was aware of a strange feeling about the house, a sort of oppressive heaviness. A bit like those breathless few hours before a really violent storm, when the very air itself seems to press on you. I was getting the same sort of headache that I got in those circumstances. I'm sensitive to atmosphere. If you'd grown up in an orphanage, you would be, too.

The wretched mayonnaise curdled again. I threw out the second batch, guiltily thinking of what a waste of good food I was making. Mrs. Cotting stirred the soup for tonight, grumbling about her sore feet. You suffer terribly with your feet when you're in service, you're always on them. Some days, I didn't sit down for hours at a time. It gave you an awfully sore back, too.

The third batch of mayonnaise mixed properly, thank goodness. I transferred it to the ice-box, taking a little longer than usual to close the lid. It was so pleasant to feel that cooler air on my face. The ice came from the manor grounds, where there was an ice-house close to the lake, in a dank little hollow, stocked each winter and chipped away for use, piece by piece, throughout the year.

"Joan, those cuffs are absolutely filthy," Mrs. Cotting said sharply, as I came back into the kitchen. I looked down at my wrists – she was right. They were splashed and marked with egg and oil and milk, coffee grounds from breakfast, and other assorted stains.

"I'm sorry. I'll go and put on my spare pair."

"Quick as you can, then."

I said a rude word in the privacy of my own head as I left the kitchen. Four flights of stairs to climb on my already aching feet and legs to reach my attic room. I don't know why I made for the main staircase, rather than using the servants' one I was supposed to take. Perhaps I rebelliously wanted to feel the plush carpet beneath my poor soles, rather than the hard old linoleum of the back stairs.

I rounded the first flight of stairs quickly and stopped dead. The mistress was standing with her back to me, twisting and wringing her hands. I must have made a sound, an intake of breath perhaps, because she swung around to face me. Her face was working and she looked as if she'd walked into something solid and was still trying to get her breath back. Her hands pulled and twisted at her sleeves.

She looked so distressed I found my arms going out instinctively, before self-preservation kicked in. "Madam?" I asked, tentatively. For a moment, I wondered whether she even saw me; her gaze was turned inward, glassy and blank like the eyes of a dead fish.

"I don't know what to do," she said. Her voice shook as if someone had hold of her by the shoulders. "I don't know what to do!"

"Madam, let me fetch someone," I said, in as soothing a voice as I could. "I'll go and find Miss Maddox..."

"No!" Her restless hands went out, as if to ward me off. Then she turned around and ran up the stairs, stumbling once and falling to her knees before picking herself up and running upwards again. I could hear her crying as she turned the corner of the corridor on the first floor.

I remained where I was for a moment. I was so shaken I'd forgotten why I was even going upstairs. Should I really fetch Miss Cleo? After a moment, I turned and walked back down the stairs, slowly. I thought I'd better take the servants' staircase, after all.

That night I wrote to Verity. It was hard to capture exactly how I was feeling, because I didn't know myself – there was an oppressive feeling of dread hanging over me, but formless, because I didn't know why I felt like that. Not for the first time, I wished I were back in London. I frowned over my writing paper, unable to articulate my thoughts. Words which would normally flow from my pen seemed to stick in the nib. In the end, I wrote: *V, I'm worried but I don't know why. I feel like something bad is about to happen but I don't know what. We must meet up soon, so you can talk some sense into me!* I signed it off as usual, with three kisses, and then added a P.S. *Don't worry about me, it's probably nothing. I'm being fanciful – as usual! Love J.*

The next day, the fine weather broke and it rained. The sky was like a sagging grey blanket spread over the manor. In the kitchen, Mrs. Cotting was in a fine mood, slamming pots and pans around and letting off a slow hissing mumble, rather like the kettle that was kept simmering on the stove top.

"Is something the matter?" I asked, rather tentatively. In my experience, asking that question is normally an invitation to have one's head bitten off.

"I'm not accustomed to having my dishes questioned. I serve nothing but good, wholesome food in here, and who's to say I don't." Mrs. Cotting bent down to shoot the Yorkshire pudding dish into the oven and slammed the door with a wrathful clang.

"Who's been asking questions?" I couldn't imagine the mistress having the temerity to take Mrs. Cotting up on anything, let alone what went on in the kitchen.

"That John Manfield!" Mrs. Cotting was annoyed enough to not use his title. "Coming down here, poking his nose in. What's he know about cooking, I'd like to know?"

"What was he asking?"

"Oh, what kind of meat was I using, how long was I cooking it for? Just because Madam's ill again. It's nothing to do with my cooking, I told him, and I'll thank him not to make my job any more difficult than it actually is."

Mrs. Cotting huffed off into the larder and I turned my attention back to the soup, stirring its murky depths. Soon I would add crushed eggs shells to it and whisk it thoroughly, skimming off every bit of froth and scum that rose to the surface. Then I would lay sheets of greaseproof paper over it, over and over again, until the soup itself was a wonderful clear golden colour, totally transparent.

At the moment, the soup was still sludgy with vegetables and bones. I stirred it gently, feeling the steam against my face and thinking about what Mrs. Cotting had said. Surely Mr. Manfield wasn't implying that the mistress was getting food poisoning? Once, perhaps (although I could never say that to Mrs. Cotting, if I valued my life), but not over and over again, surely? Perhaps she wasn't able to eat something we kept cooking without being ill? I knew a girl like that in the orphanage; if she ate eggs, she'd come over all queer and be violently ill.

Not that we got many eggs in the orphanage, you can be sure of that, so it wasn't really a problem.

That night, the master went up to London, as he did frequently for the start of the week. With just the mistress, her brother, Miss Cleo and Mrs. Carter-Knox to worry about, it was a more peaceful evening than we'd had for a while. It rained steadily all afternoon and the night seemed to draw in quicker than usual. When I went out to fetch some milk from the dairy, I noticed, for the first time, the leaves on the trees by the gate were touched with the first autumnal hints. By six o'clock, it was almost as dark as it would be in October.

I was wearily putting away the last of the silver into the silver cabinet when I heard one of the bells ringing. It's not rightly my job to answer them, but Mrs. Cotting had already retired and Meg was off fetching wood for the stove, so I went into the corridor as quickly as my tired legs would allow. The bell to the Blue Room was bouncing and jangling on its wire: Mr. Manfield's room. I thought of the stairs between here and the second floor and groaned, but made my way to the staircase nonetheless.

Mr. Manfield's room was next to the master's, which was next to the mistress's room. I hesitated briefly outside her door as I could hear the faint murmur of voices within. Then I knocked on Mr. Manfield's door.

After a few minutes, I knocked again. After a

moment, Madam's door opened and Mr. Manfield came out. He looked worried. Miss Cleo followed him out a moment later. She was frowning slightly.

"Oh, hello Joan," he said, clearly not wondering why I was answering the bells and not the housemaid. It was all the same to him. Miss Cleo shut the bedroom door carefully behind her. "We're just getting my sister settled. She should be fine, now. Do you think you could bring me some hot milk? I'm just about in and I could do with a good night's sleep."

"Yes, of course, sir. Should I make you some cocoa or is it just the milk you want?"

"That's dashed kind of you, but milk is fine."

"I'll bring it straight up, sir."

"Darling, would you make me one too?" asked Miss Cleo, abruptly. I was faintly surprised – she didn't normally touch milky drinks. It was normally gin or champagne all the way for her.

"Yes, of course, Madam." I bobbed a quick curtsey and turned away.

I was just going back down the stairs when I thought I heard the faint sound of someone calling me. I hesitated, one foot on the top stairs, listening with held breath. There was nothing. I was on the verge of walking down when I found myself turning around and hurrying back to the door of Madam's room. I knocked tentatively and when no one answered, I carefully pushed open the door.

I didn't know what I was doing or why I was being so forward. It was almost as if there was something unseen tugging me into the room, like a little hand in mine, pulling me forward insistently.

Madam was in bed, her face turned towards the door, the covers drawn up to just under her shoulders. Her delicate hands clutched the top of the silk eiderdown. I thought she was asleep but, as I crept forward, her eyes snapped open suddenly, although I'd made no sound.

"Madam?" I asked tentatively. "Shall I – can I bring you anything? Did you call?"

She continued to stare at me, her eyes heavy-lidded and her pupils large and dark like sloes. I wondered whether she'd actually been asleep and I'd awakened her. I braced myself for anger but, after a moment, she smiled a sweet smile and shook her head, quite insistently, like a child.

"You don't want anything?" I persisted. What was wrong with me? I could feel that same uneasiness I'd felt all week, incongruous in this beautifully decorated, luxurious bedchamber.

Madam smiled and shook her head again, less forcefully this time. I had the uneasy feeling that she didn't actually know who I was. But what else could I do? I bobbed a curtsey and said a limp, "Goodnight then, Madam," and made my way back out in the corridor, shutting the door behind me. I ran down the stairs, feeling as breathless as if I were running up them.

Meg was back in the kitchen when I got back. I took two mugs from the hooks on the dresser and made up the hot drink. "Here, take this up to Mr. Manfield for me, Meg. He's off to bed and wants something to help him sleep. Take one for Miss Cleo, too."

Meg leapt at the chance, as I knew she would. She was sweet on him, poor girl, as if anything would ever come of that.

Mrs. Smith came into the kitchen to fill the kettle from her room. I opened my mouth to ask whether she thought Madam was really any better and then shut it again. I didn't want to mention that I'd asked Madam if she needed any help – it wasn't really my place to have done that. All I could say to myself was that I'd been worried.

I slept badly that night. Annie snored like a pig and the air in the room felt like a warm, dusty blanket, pressing down over my face. After waking three times, I got up and crossly looked out some cotton wool to put in my ears. Knowing that you'll be exhausted before the day even starts is a horrible thing. Eventually I fell into a thin sleep, muddied with strange dreams.

When it was time to get up for work, I dragged myself, groaning, out of bed; normally it was so uncomfortable but this morning it felt like the softest feather mattress in the world. I splashed cold water on my face in a vain attempt to make myself feel more awake. Tucking my hair up underneath my cap and pinning it there, I clumped downstairs. Mrs. Cotting was in the larder, marking up a list for the delivery boy. I stopped in the kitchen doorway, blinking. My head felt stuffed with fog after my bad night but, for a second, I felt a jab of unease, like a silvery pinprick of light through the clouds of tiredness. *There was something wrong.*

I blinked again and the feeling went, buried under a wave of tiredness. I yawned hugely. One of the luxuries of Asharton Manor was a pot of coffee for the staff every morning and I made my way straight to the stove, pouring myself a generous cup. That silvery dart of anxiety pierced me again. What *was* wrong? I was too tired to think. I gave myself an irritable shake and turned my attention to making breakfast.

I was drooping over the frying pan, turning the sizzling slices of bacon, when the kitchen door banged back on its hinges and Violet came rushing into the kitchen, wringing her hands and gibbering. We all stared at her in astonishment; me at the stove, Mrs. Cotting by the larder, and Mrs. Smith sorting through the laundry receipts at her desk in the corner of the room.

"What on Earth—" Mrs. Smith said as Violet

rushed over to her, her hands up in her hair, pulling it out from the pins.

"It's Madam, it's Madam – oh, Mrs. Smith, it's awful – she's lying there all cold, there's something wrong – all *cold* – I think she's dead—"

Talk about cold. A drenching, chilly wave washed over me, just as I gasped and I heard Mrs. Cotting do the same.

Mrs. Smith just stared blankly. "What on Earth are you talking about, Violet?"

"Madam's dead, I think she's dead!"

Meg, who was setting bread at the kitchen table, gave a short sharp scream. We all jumped and Mrs. Smith got up quickly. "Dead? Don't be ridiculous!"

Violet was still moaning and crying. Mrs Cotting drew her over to a chair and sat her down. She, Mrs Smith and I looked at each other, silently wondering.

"Joan, come with me," Mrs. Smith said, finally. She and Mrs. Cotting exchanged another quick glance and Mrs. Cotting nodded very slightly. Violet had sunk her head into her hands and both she and Meg were crying. I think Mrs. Smith wanted someone she could rely on to accompany her. If I was capable of thinking anything, I was pleased, but my heart was thumping. I thought of that silvery dart of anxiety that I'd felt walking into the kitchen. Had I had a premonition?

We walked quickly up the main staircase. I

knew then that Mrs. Smith was worried, because we would normally have taken the servants' stairs. We reached the landing, where Madam's door stood ajar. Mrs. Smith hesitated on the landing. Then – I could hear her take a deep breath – she walked inside the room and I followed her.

The bedside light was on and the tea tray deposited on the table next to the bed. Madam lay in bed like a marble statue. I could see at first glance that she was dead; her mouth hung open and there was a greyish tinge to her skin, as if she'd walked through a room full of dust and cobwebs. I could smell it too – death smells like nothing else, sweet and rank at the same time. I swallowed.

"Oh, my lord," said Mrs. Smith, breathing fast. "Oh, my lord. Oh Joan... oh, my lord..."

I looked at her in alarm. She was very pale, with a sheen of perspiration over her face like a transparent veil.

"Quick—" I said and got her to a chair just in time. I helped her put her head near her ample lap, wishing I had some smelling salts. I looked at the dressing table, thinking I might see some there, but the light was too dim and the table too far away in the enormous room for me to see clearly.

"Wait here, I'll get help," I said. Mrs. Smith said something muffled in reply, but I didn't stop to ask her to repeat it. I ran quickly to the door and down the corridor to Mr. Manfield's room and knocked before I had a chance to think about what I was doing.

It seemed an age before I heard a sleepy voice say, "Come in." I almost fell into the room, such was my haste – I didn't stop to think what he might think of me, a servant, barging into his bedchamber without so much as a by your leave. As I opened my mouth to gasp out the news, I realised what I was about to say. I was about to tell him his sister was dead.

"What's that?" he asked, as if he couldn't just believe what he'd heard.

I had to repeat myself, this time at least remembering to add, "I'm so sorry, sir."

Mr. Manfield got slowly out of bed and reached for his gown. I hastily dropped my eyes.

"Did I hear you correctly?" he asked. He put one hand up to his face and I could see his fingers shaking. "Did I?"

"I'm so sorry," I said desperately. "Please, will you come with me, sir?"

When we got back into the room, Mrs. Smith had raised her head. She still looked deathly pale, but her breathing had steadied a little.

Mr. Manfield gasped when he saw the still figure on the bed. He didn't say anything else. For a moment, the three of us looked on in silence.

The door opened behind us and made all three of us jump. Miss Cleo came into the room, rubbing her face, her dark flapper bob tousled from sleep.

"What's going on?" she said sleepily and then caught sight of Mrs. Denford. Her hand went to her mouth. After a moment, she wheeled around and walked blindly out of the room, rebounding off the doorway as she misjudged the distance. I could hear her footsteps running down the corridor and the faint sound of retching before the bathroom door slammed. After a moment, I could also hear Mrs. Carter-Knox calling faintly and querulously from her bedroom. For the moment, we all ignored her

"We need to call a doctor," said Mr. Manfield eventually and I leapt at the opportunity to do just that; anything to get out of the room filled with absence.

The time in a house after a death is strange. Everything is muffled, but at the same time, individual noises are too loud. I dropped a saucepan when I was preparing lunch and the clang of it on the stone flags sent both me and Mrs. Cotting shooting into the air like fireworks. I'd worked in two houses before where someone had died. The first – and the worst – was one of the Jewish places I'd worked, where a newborn baby had smothered in its sleep, one night. Oh my goodness, that was a terrible time – even this horrible event at Asharton didn't compare to *that*. No one in that house stopped crying for a week after it happened, servants and gentry alike. The second was another London place; there, the master's brother had died after a long illness. He'd been gassed in the Great War and never really recovered. That was sad, but he'd been ill for so long that no one was really very shocked. As I chopped onions, wiping my eyes with my cuffs, I wondered whether that was the case here. Madam had been ill, after all, for months. Was that why she had died? It must be. *It must be*, I repeated to myself, in the privacy of my head, wondering whether I was trying to convince myself.

Mrs. Cotting and I prepared lunch but no one was very interested in eating. We sat picking at our food and exchanging desultory remarks about nothing in particular. The mistress's death hung over us all, but no one dared to mention it. We'd seen the doctor's car drive off with a black hospital van behind him and knew that the mistress was taking her final trip from Asharton. I hadn't been in the room when the doctor had arrived and I longed to ask Mrs, Smith what he had said, but knew that I couldn't.

The master arrived back on the express train that afternoon. We were all lined up in the hallway as he came through the front door, our hands clasped in front of us, our eyes demurely lowered. My gaze flickered up as he walked past me; his face was shut tight, like a locked box. I wondered what he was thinking or feeling. Had he loved his wife? Was he sorry that she was dead? I remembered her hissed remark to him at the dinner table that night. Was he sorry that she had gone or did he feel something more akin to relief? It was impossible to tell and I was thankful that no one around me could read my mind (or at least I hoped). I was burning to write to Verity and tell her everything, but work went on and, despite the gloom on the house, meals still had to be prepared, dishes washed, supplies ordered and everything made neat and ready for tomorrow.

Again, I was the last one in the kitchen that night. Normally, that didn't bother me but today I felt terribly jumpy, starting at the creaking of the floorboards in the rooms above me, jumping as the tinkle of a teaspoon in the sink sounded as loud as a clashing cymbal. I decided to make myself a mug of cocoa to take up to bed with me. It was as I was reaching for one of the cups on the row of hooks on the dresser that I realised what had been bothering me all day.

The cups. The cups were wrong – or had been wrong - this morning, when I'd first walked into the kitchen. It seemed like a long time ago now, but I could still clearly recall that dart of unease, the sense of something being not quite right that I'd felt as I entered the room. And now I knew why. There should have been two cups missing this morning – the mugs I'd given to Meg to give to Mr. Manfield and Miss Cleo, filled with hot milk. But – I could see it plain as day in my memory – all the cups had been on the hooks, first thing this morning.

I made my cocoa and took it upstairs with me, frowning through the steam as I carried it all the way up the servants' stairs. Why had those cups been put back? Not just washed up, but dried and hung back with the others? I reached my room, thankful that Annie was asleep already. I put my hand out to put on the bedside light, but something stopped me. I sipped my cocoa in the dark, tucked beneath the blankets, thinking hard.

Meg must have collected the cups before she went to bed. Surely? That was the simplest explanation – but I knew it was wrong. Meg, sweet on Mr. Manfield as she had been, would never have gone back to his room after he retired for the night. Nor would any of the other servants. Even the valet that Mr. Manfield shared with the master wouldn't have deigned to bring a cup down to the kitchen if he'd seen it – let alone wash it, dry it and hang it up. So who had it been? Surely not Mr. Manfield himself? Friendly as he was to the servants, I could not see him even thinking to do such a mundane, domestic thing, let alone doing it. Why was Miss Cleo's mug here as well? Had she brought both cups down to the kitchen? Why would she? I couldn't see it happening.

I turned it over in my mind, trying to see how it could have happened, and more importantly, *why*. It was so late, I was so tired, but my mind would not let me rest. I felt that same strange pulling sensation as I had when I stood outside Madam's door, the night before. The night she had died. *"Stop thinking about it,"* I whispered to myself. *"There's nothing you can do now."* I put the empty cocoa cup down on the floor and wriggled further beneath the covers, shivering.

I WOKE UP EARLY THE next morning, despite a bad night's sleep. I lit the stub of candle by my bed, reached for my writing paper and began a frantic letter for Verity. I was almost out of writing paper, so I crossed the sheet and put as much detail down as I could in the small amount of space that I had. It had crossed my mind to send a telegram but I didn't have that much money, and I knew Verity would worry if she received one. It wasn't as if I could put a lot of detail into a telegram. Instead, I wrote. *I must see you, V – is there any way we can manage to meet up? Perhaps halfway between here and London? I need your help and advice.*

At breakfast that morning, Violet was the one bold enough to ask what we were all wanting to know. "What did the doctor say, Mr. Pettigrew? Why did Madam die?"

Mr. Pettigrew harrumphed. He looked as though he was going to reprove Violet for her curiosity, but then he caught the eye of Mrs. Smith and probably came to the conclusion that we may as well know.

"The doctor is of the opinion that Madam had a sudden attack of the illness that she's been suffering, a severe attack."

"Is that all?" Violet said, the disappointment obvious in her voice. She caught Mrs. Smith's eye and flushed.

After breakfast, I asked Meg if she'd cleared away the cups she'd taken up to Mr. Manfield and Miss Cleo that night. She shook her head, mystified at my asking. "Why, Joan?"

"It doesn't matter," I said. I began to hang the saucepans back on their hooks, my hands moving automatically. Why did I feel it mattered so much? *She died of natural causes,* I told myself. *The doctor said so.*

When the police arrived that afternoon, it didn't come as the shock it should have. I think part of me had been prepared for this, ever since it had happened. We clustered downstairs, whispering, while Mrs. Smith clumped upstairs, her face set, to receive them.

"I told you," Violet whispered triumphantly, if you can do such a thing. "She done away with herself. It's obvious."

In fact, Violet had said no such thing.

"Don't be stupid," I said, slightly more sharply than I'd intended. Violet flushed up to her eyebrows – a most unbecoming colour - and she was opening her lips to retort when Mrs. Cotting came bustling up to break up our little huddle.

"Come on, gels, back to your work. There's nothing more to be learned here. Go on, on with you." We hesitated and she said, as if something she'd learned by rote, "The police always have to come if it's an unexpected death. Nothing more to it than that. Go on, now."

We drifted back to our work, unwillingly. I wondered how Mrs. Cotting knew that for a fact. It sounded as it if were something she'd been told and she was merely repeating it, word for word. I tried to remember if the police had come to either of the deaths I'd experienced before, but I genuinely couldn't remember. I was so tired.

VERITY WROTE BACK TO ME by return of post. Quickly, I scanned her words and saw that she'd suggested a date in the next week to meet in London. I put the letter against my forehead, closing my eyes in thankfulness. I could make the day she'd suggested. The thought of seeing Verity again, of being able to unload all of my worries, was like a warm bath at the end of a long day. Before I did anything else, I scribbled on a postcard that we would do exactly as suggested, that I would meet her at Paddington. I'd had so little time off lately, what with all the disruption, that I knew Mrs.

Cotting would agree to me staying away overnight. I added a P.S. to my note to Verity: *I cannot wait to see you. Things are very bad here and I desperately need to talk to someone.* After a moment, I slipped the postcard into an envelope, not wanting anyone else's eyes to see what I had written.

A WEEK LATER, I WAS stepped down from my train at Paddington Station and, looking up through the clouds of dirty steam, saw Verity waiting for me on the platform. A bubble of gladness almost lifted me off my feet. She flung her arms about me and kissed me on both cheeks. Then we stood back a little, appraising one another.

"You're awfully pale," she scolded.

"Oh, V, I am so pleased to see you." It wasn't like me but, for a moment, I thought I was going to burst into tears. "I can't tell you what an awful time it's been."

She tucked her arm into mine and began to gently pull me towards the exit. "Let's go and have tea and cake and you can tell me all about it."

We did just that. She let me talk and talk I did, the words pouring out of me just as the tea poured from the pot. I didn't actually eat much cake, I was too busy talking. Verity didn't say much but listened intently, frowning occasionally.

"What do the police think?" was the first thing that she asked, when I finally managed to shut up.

"I don't know. But they did do a – what do they call it? A post mortem."

"What was the result?"

"They didn't find anything to show how she might have died. No arsenic, or anything like that."

"Hmm," said Verity. "What do you think?"

I put my cup down and twisted it in the saucer. "I don't know either," I confessed. "But something's not right. Those cups..."

"Yes," said Verity, frowning again. "I can see why that worries you."

I picked up my cup and then put it down again. "Why would someone wash up a cup and put it back in the kitchen, unless they didn't want anyone to notice that it had been used?"

Verity topped up my cup with the last of the tea. "Exactly," she said.

We looked at one another.

"Who could have done such a thing?" I asked, not really wanting the answer.

Verity smiled. "It's normally the husband, isn't it?" she said. "You told me they quarrelled all the time. Perhaps he just wanted her out of the way."

"I suppose so." I smiled back. "But he wasn't there. He was away for the night, in London. This isn't one of your plays, you know. People don't really do such things in real life. Do they?"

"You tell me," Verity said cynically. "Anyway, talking of plays, I've got tickets for us to go tonight."

I clapped my hands together in delight. "That's wonderful, V. I haven't been to the theatre since I left London. Oh, it's just what I need to take my mind off it all."

Verity giggled. "You might not think that when you find out what the play is. 'Death at the Manor'! It's a farce, though, not a real mystery."

I laughed too. "Well, I can't wait. Is it at the Chelsea Palladium?"

"Yes. And we can go backstage, as well. My uncle is playing the lead."

Verity's mother had been an actress, too. I remember when Verity told me about her parents, back when we were in the orphanage. Her father had been a minor aristocrat, second cousin to the king's nephew, twice removed - that sort of thing. He'd fallen in love with Verity's mother after watching her act and they'd eloped to Gretna Green, much to the shame and horror of his family, who'd promptly disowned him. So, despite the grand history, Verity's family's fortunes went down and down and culminated in her father blowing his brains out with his revolver, just before the war, unable to face the shame of his debts and the terror of the upcoming battle. Verity's mother had died in the influenza epidemic of 1918, leaving Verity an orphan.

I'm ashamed to say that when I first heard her

family's tragic history, the first words out of my mouth were something like, "All my eye and Betty Martin! Pull the other one, it's got bells on." I can't tell you how bad I felt when I found out it was all true. That was partly why Verity was so well read – both her mother and her father had insisted on good schooling for her; she'd even had a governess, at one point. And now she was working as a housemaid. There were those who would have been crushed by this reversal of fortune, but not Verity. She was clever and capable and she had big plans. I hoped I could be right beside her, all the way; she made me proud.

We had a gay time at the theatre and, for a while, I forgot Asharton Manor and the smell of death and the mystery of the mugs. The play was a silly thing, but amusing, and afterwards, as Verity had promised, we went backstage to meet the actors. I'd met Verity's uncle, Tommy, before; her late mother's younger brother was a hoot, full of charm and jokes and with Verity's red hair. He introduced us to another cast member, Ashley Turton, whose performance – and person – we'd admired from our seats. He was quieter than Tommy, but just as nice. He reminded me of someone, but I couldn't think who it could be. It would come to me later, no doubt.

"My, that Ashley's handsome," I said to Verity on the bus home afterwards. "A new beau for you?"

She gave me a strange look, half a smile and half a frown. "Hardly, Joan," she said. Then she laughed a little. "He wouldn't be interested in me!"

"Why not?" I asked, indignant on her behalf. Verity's not exactly what you would call beautiful, but she's got something. She's the sort of person you like to look at.

Verity laughed harder. "Take it from me, Joan, he really wouldn't be interested. He's one of *those*."

The penny dropped and I blushed. "Oh, I see," I said. Then I laughed too. "What a waste."

I stayed in Verity's room that night, top-to-tail in her bed, as we usually did. Edna, who shared her room, was away for the night visiting her mother so it was nice to talk uninterrupted, although we had to keep our voices down – difficult, as we had so much to talk about. At first we talked of the play and our work, but gradually, inevitably, talk drifted back to the death at Asharton Manor. Verity made me tell her what had happened again, from the moment I arrived at the manor to the moment I got on the train to come up to London. I thought hard, and spoke slowly, trying not to leave anything out.

"Do you think she could have killed herself?" Verity asked, once I'd finished speaking.

I lifted my shoulders in the darkness. "I don't know. I remember coming across her on the stairs that day – she looked so desperate. I suppose she might have done."

"But if she did do away with herself, how did she do it? And another thing... perhaps she looked desperate because she'd just had a horrible shock? Didn't she say to you 'I don't know what to do?' That suggests to me that she'd found something out and she didn't know what to do about it."

"Yes, I suppose you're right," I said, slowly.

"Who inherits her money?"

"Oh, V, how would I know? Her husband, I suppose."

"I could find out."

"Really?" I was intrigued. "How?"

"I could go to Somerset House."

I yawned. Much as I wanted to continue the conversation, I was fighting a losing battle against sleep. "Why don't you do that?" I murmured and yawned again. "At least we'd know. Thanks, V."

She said nothing but I could feel her give my leg an affectionate pat as I fell forward into unconsciousness.

WE SAID GOODBYE EARLY THE next morning at the station. I felt so much better for having shared my worries; I felt as if I'd been away for a week, not just a night.

"Take care of yourself, Joanie," said Verity, hugging me.

"You too."

She held me at arm's length and looked at me gravely. "No, I mean, *take care of yourself*. Don't tell anyone what you've told me – about the cups or the mistress having a shock. Not *anyone*. Understand?"

"Yes," I said, a little shaken by her firmness. Then the penny dropped. "Oh goodness, V, you don't think I'm actually in danger, do you?"

Verity shrugged. She stepped back a little and adjusted her gloves. "I don't know, Joan, but let's be on the safe side, shall we? I can't lose you. What would we do without one another?"

We smiled at each other affectionately. The train hooted and I jumped.

"Better get aboard," said Verity. "I'll write very soon."

"Me too."

We waved as the train pulled out and I tried not to mind too much. Her last words to me kept recurring. *Don't tell anyone*. That meant she thought that – well, that someone in the house was responsible for Madam's death. I leant back into my third class seat, biting my lip and looking out the window, unseeing. Verity thought someone in that house was a murderer.

For the first time since the death, I allowed myself to acknowledge that fact. Because hadn't that been at the back of my mind all this time? But who could it be? And why? The guard slammed the carriage door open, bellowing for tickets, and I jumped a foot in the air. Once he'd clipped my ticket and gone, I tried to think again, but my thoughts had been scattered.

I had no money for a taxi from the station at Midford and, of course, they hadn't sent a car for me. I managed to hitch a ride for part of the way home, on the back of a farm wagon laden with turnips; a fine sight I must have been, perched up on the side, trying to keep my feet out of the muddy root vegetables stacked on the floor of the cart. I didn't actually mind too much; I had more than dirty shoes on my mind. As we drew closer to Asharton Manor, I could feel my apprehensiveness increase. The farmer dropped me off about a mile from the manor and I walked the rest of the way, swapping my overnight bag from one aching hand to the other. As I walked up the long driveway and rounded the long, swooping corner, the house gradually revealed itself to me and I felt a qualm of pure fear. Behind it, the pine forest stood, black and menacing. I remembered the grove where Astarte's temple had stood. Human sacrifice.... I shivered and, for a moment, put down my bag and stared. Why had I taken the job here, of all places? Why couldn't I have stayed in London, where at least I would have been safe?

There was still a subdued feel about the house. I gave Annie the film magazine I'd brought back with me from London and she thanked me nicely, but without the squeal of delight she'd have given a week ago. Mrs. Cotting merely nodded and said, "You're back, then," to which there really isn't any answer, is there? She'd kept some cottage pie from lunch back for me though, so the grudgingness of her welcome was outweighed by her thoughtfulness in doing that.

I threw myself back into work with a fervour that surprised me (and delighted Mrs. Cotting). I know now I was trying to avoid thinking too deeply. Of course, with the house in mourning and one less person to feed, the menus were a lot less complicated than they had been. I found myself helping Meg scour the copper pans at one point, a truly horrid job, but it was better than standing about idle. Also, I wanted to see what had been happening since I'd been away.

"Have the police been back?" I asked quietly as we sat together in the scullery, rubbing the salt paste in industrially.

Meg nodded, her mouth crimped. "They were shut up with the master for ever so long."

"But they left again?" What I meant was, did they leave without arresting him?

Meg nodded again. "Oh yes. Said they might be back, but didn't say when."

"They didn't take the master with them?" I checked to be sure.

"Oh, no. He went upstairs afterwards for a rest. He was fair worn out."

"Who else did they question?"

"Mr. Manfield. They were with him for a little while. And Miss Cleo, and Mrs. Carter-Knox. Everyone, really. They even asked to speak to Mrs. Smith and Mr. Pettigrew."

"Did you have to talk to them?"

Meg shook her head, clearly thankful.

The next morning, there was a letter for me, from Verity –just a short, one-page scribble. *I've been to Somerset House. Mrs. Denford left most of her estate to her husband, a little bit to her brother, her jewellery to Cleo Maddox and some small bequests to some of the servants. Not you, Joanie, worst luck!* I smiled at that. *Just one more thing, before I sign off. Where in Africa did Mr. Manfield have his ranch? Can you find out for me? Thanks – it's important. And remember, not a word to anyone. Hide this letter. Yours ever, Verity.*

I folded the letter away carefully and hid it in my summer shoes, which were packed away in a dusty corner of the wardrobe in my room. What on Earth did Verity mean about Africa? I mentally shrugged and wondered how I would find out.

I was walking towards the compost bin outside the back door, a bowl of carrot peelings in my hand, when I glanced up and saw the black swathe of the pine forest beyond the buildings of the manor. It reminded me of that day I got lost in the woods, when I found the grove of Astarte's temple. I came to a sudden stop, drawing in my breath. I realised that I did actually know the answer to Verity's question. I thought back to the conversation that Mr Manfield and I had had there. What had he said? *I lived on the east coast, a place called Teganka...*

I wrote back to Verity that evening. I still wasn't quite sure why she wanted to know. After I'd sealed and addressed the envelope and placed it in on my bedside table, I stretched and yawned. The yellow candlelight flickered.

"Writing to your friend?" asked Annie.

"Yes." I looked across at her. She was sitting with her knees up and her nightdress tucked under her feet, like a little girl, reading the film magazine I'd brought her from London. I let my gaze drift up to the wall beyond her bed and my eyes rested on all the cut out pictures of the stars. It must be a strange life, being an actor. I thought of Verity's uncle and of his friend, Ashley Turton. It was then I realised who Ashley Turton reminded me of.

It was such a strange thought, so unexpected, that my mind wanted to reject it. *Don't be silly, Joan*, I told myself in my head. But the thought – no, the knowledge was there, inescapable. How did I know? I just did.

A little shaken, I lay down in bed and turned over to face the wall. Why had this knowledge shaken me? Did it actually matter? I tried to dismiss the thought, closing my eyes and pretending to sleep, as if I could fool myself into actually doing so.

I was hard at work a few days later, dealing with the aftermath of breakfast, when Mr. Pettigrew appeared in the doorway of the kitchen, his formidable eyebrows pitched so high that they almost disappeared into his combed back hair.

"There is a telephone call," he said ponderously. "For Joan."

"For me?" I straightened up in shock. Who on Earth would be calling me?

"What on Earth—" Mrs. Cotting pinched her mouth together and shook her head. "I don't know what your friends are thinking of, Joan, ringing you up on the telephone."

"I don't know, either," I said, honestly. If I hadn't been an orphan, I would have been worried. Surely only a death in the family would have warranted a telephone call. "May I go?"

I could feel waves of disapproval buffeting me from both Mr. Pettigrew and Mrs. Cotting but, after a moment, she inclined her head in a snappish little nod. *I'll pay for this*, I thought, as I climbed the stairs to the hallway, but I was too concerned - too intrigued by the thought of my telephone call - to be really worried about the repercussions.

The telephone stood on the hallway table over by the staircase. It was dwarfed by one of Mrs.

Carter-Knox's monstrous flower arrangements. I picked up the receiver and disentangled myself from a wayward plant tendril which had caught on my hair.

It was Verity, of course. I should have known.

"What are you doing?" I hissed down the receiver. I think it was the first time we'd ever actually spoken on the telephone. Her voice sounded strange, high and excited.

"Listen, Joanie, I didn't have a choice. This is really important. Are you alone? Can anyone overhear you?"

I glanced around the hallway. It was a shadowy place, with the only light coming from the windows at the front, by the huge front door. The chandelier blazed overhead but the light it cast was dappled and strange.

"Go ahead," I said, quietly.

"I went to the British Library and read up everything I could on Tenganka."

"Who?"

"Not who. A place in Africa."

"Oh, yes," I said, remembering. I glanced back behind me again but there was nobody there. "But why?"

Verity rushed on breathlessly. "When you were telling me about meeting Mr. Manfield in the woods, he told you something about a local tribe -

in Tenganka - that had a superstition. They used to ill wish people, who then died – remember?"

I nodded and then realised that was ridiculous. "Yes, I remember."

"Well," said Verity. "I found some research papers, by a team of scientists who were studying the flora and fauna in the area. They found that the seeds from the Henget tree – which is also known as the 'sickness tree' - which grows in Tenganka, can induce sickness and delirium in a person and can cause death, if given in sufficient quantities." It sounded as though she was reading from a page of notes. "The scientists found that the tribes who had this superstition actually used these seeds to make people unwell. So it was really happening, not because of something supernatural."

"Very well," I said again, rather helplessly. "But why—"

"Oh, Joanie, you comprehend, don't you? Who at Asharton Manor kept being unwell and then getting better and then being unwell again?"

"Oh," I said, knowledge dawning. I swallowed. "Do you really think that's what's happened?"

"Well, I don't know for sure," confessed Verity. "But it's a sight odd, isn't it? The brother turns up from Africa, straight from this place where he knows how these seeds are used to make people ill, and then all of a sudden, his sister's horribly unwell?"

"It could be a coincidence," I said, feebly.

"Well, it might." Verity didn't sound convinced.

"He's not the only person who's been to Africa," I said suddenly, remembering. "Mrs. Carter-Knox lived there, too. She might have known about the sickness tree."

"Right," said Verity. "The other thing is—" She hesitated. "The other thing is, I can't see why they would do it? What's in it for them? Mrs. Denford didn't leave anything to her aunt and hardly anything to her brother. I suppose he – Mr. Manfield - might have hated her, but that didn't seem to be the case did it? I—"

I talked across her, feverishly. A firework of possibilities had just gone off in my head, shooting stars of red and green and blue. "Verity, I know. I think I know who killed her. But I need to prove it."

"How will you do that?"

"I don't know, yet. Listen, is there any way – any way at all – that you could come here? I know you've just had a day off, but I need you to help me."

Verity half laughed. "Well, I could try the old 'my great aunt is sick' excuse. I've covered for Mrs. Antells, on occasion. I think I could talk her around. I could only come for the day, though."

"If you could be here, that would be wonderful. I don't think I can go to the police without – well, without evidence."

"I'll come. I'll do my utmost. Listen, I've got to

go and so should you. I'll let you know when I can catch the train to you."

"Thank you," I said and I meant it from the bottom of my heart. We said goodbye and I put the receiver down. I stared up at the glittering chandelier for a moment, through the luxuriant growth of the flower arrangement. Was what I was thinking really likely? There was a part of me that wanted to reject the thought, and I knew why. But suppose I was right? What was I going to do? What would be the moral thing - the ethical thing - to do? I had my nails in my mouth, nibbling in anxiety. Then I saw Mr. Pettigrew walking toward me from the end of the hallway, disapproval written all over his face. I bobbed a quick curtsey and scurried back to the kitchen.

THAT NIGHT, I LAY IN bed in the darkness, wide-eyed. I could hear Annie breathing softly across the room. I turned over in bed, trying not to make too much noise.

It wasn't even as if I'd even liked the mistress much – I hadn't. But I couldn't forget that feeling of a tiny hand pushing me towards her bedroom door the night she'd died. I knew something was wrong then, that it was a silent cry for help, but I hadn't understood in time. Now I did understand and it was up to me to right that wrong. It was up to me to see justice was done.

I slid stealthily out of bed and dressed myself in the dark – just my dark blue dress, dark stockings, no shoes. I twisted my hair back off my face and pinned it back as best I could in the dark, without the aid of a mirror. Then I crept to the door and opened it as quietly as the creaky handle would allow. I tried to think of some excuse as to why I was wandering about outside my room that would sound plausible if I were seen. I couldn't really think of anything and yet I had to have something. If I was discovered then I was likely to be instantly dismissed. And – although I tried not to think of it – if the person I was looking for discovered me, then dismissal was the least of my worries. I shivered, as much from fear as from the chill of the unheated corridor.

I crept downstairs, using the servants' staircase. When it came to leave it, I could feel my knees tremble. At least here, on the scuffed linoleum, I was relatively safe... Leave it I did, though, and I crept forward, moving soundlessly over the plush carpet in my stocking feet, hardly breathing. My eyes had adjusted to the darkness – I had always had good night vision. I knew where I would hide – in the shadow of the grandfather clock on the landing. There was a small table there and the space between the two made a small recess I could squeeze into. I would be able to see the bedroom door clearly.

I reached the landing, reached the recess, pressed myself back into the shadows. My heart was hammering so loudly I wondered, for a second, whether anyone would be able to hear it. Gradually, as my breathing slowed, the thumping and rushing of the blood in my ears subsided. I waited, uncomfortably, for long, long minutes. After what felt like nearly an hour, I was getting angry with myself. *This was a stupid idea, Joan. You've no real evidence for thinking what you think. Just push off and go back to be—*

There was a click and a squeak from down the hallway – a bedroom lock going back, a handle turning. I forgot to breathe again, pressing myself back against the panelling of the wall. I could see a dim shape emerge from the bedroom down the hallway and creep along the passageway, just as I myself had crept from the staircase.

I pressed myself back into the shadows. I was suddenly terrified, and with good reason. This was a person who I knew had killed once before. I held my breath, dropped my gaze so what little light there was wouldn't shine off my eyes, and prayed that the booming of my heart couldn't be heard.

The stealthy footsteps crept past me. I didn't dare breathe until they stopped at the end of the corridor. There was another click as the other bedroom door opened, a tiny creak as it shut and the whisper of the bolt being pushed home. I let out my held breath in a muted gasp. I waited a few minutes, just in case. Then I pushed myself upright, wincing at the soreness in my cramped muscles. I walked carefully down the corridor, my own footsteps as stealthy as the ones I'd just heard go by. Then I stopped outside the bedroom door, inclining my head to listen.

Even though I was expecting it, the faint noises from within made my face go hot. I wished there was some way of capturing what I was hearing but, of course, there wasn't. It was enough just to confirm to myself that my suspicion had been correct. I listened for a moment longer, cheeks burning. Then I crept away again, back up the stairs to my room. I bolted the door.

Verity's train got in at ten o'clock the next day. She must have left Lord Carthright's before dawn to be able to make it down here in that time. I was grateful. I'd managed to get to the station to meet her, under the guise of doing some errands for Mrs. Cotting. The duck eggs, sausage meat and herbs were packed away in my basket and I stood on the station platform, waiting for Verity as she'd waited for me at Paddington in London.

She practically jumped onto the platform and flung her arms around me in a fierce hug. Then she released me and stood back. Her eyes searched my face. "Did you find out what you needed to?"

"Oh yes," I said. I wanted to blush again at the memory, but I fought it down. "I'll tell you all about it on the way to the manor. It's a bit of a walk, I'm afraid."

"Don't worry," said Verity stoutly. "I'm not afraid of a country walk or two."

We set off, the basket swinging between us. I told her everything that I knew or had surmised, as quickly and as quietly as possible. She didn't say much – her eyes widened at one point – but I could see her quick mind turning the possibilities over.

"There's something else," I said.

"Oh yes?"

"I've got you down here for a bit of a busman's holiday, I'm afraid."

Verity looked over at me, clearly puzzled. "Why's that, Joan?"

"If I lent you a uniform, do you think you could pretend to be – well, staff?"

Verity laughed out loud. "Seriously? Yes, of course I could. What's your housekeeper going to say, though?"

"We'll have to risk it," I said. "Perhaps we can say that you're a cousin of mine and you wanted some experience..."

I trailed off, half amused at the thought. We were walking off the road now, along a footpath that ran alongside the river. I could hear it chattering and burbling to itself as we walked along.

"And why?" Verity continued. "What do you want me to do?"

"I want you to search a room."

That brought her up short. "Really?"

I glanced around. There was nobody in sight of us. I beckoned and sat us down on a handy log by the side of the path.

"Listen," I said in a low voice. "There's no point going to the police, now. We don't have a shred of proof. But if we could find definite evidence, we could take it to the police station. Then they would have to listen to us."

"Yes," said Verity, frowning. After a moment, her frown cleared. "At least I know where all the hiding places are! I've tidied and dusted enough rooms."

"Well, quite," I said. "You know, V, it's occurred to me that we actually have a bit of an advantage over the police. You know what we're always told, about being the perfect servant..."

"'We have to be invisible,'" Verity chanted, remembering our training at the orphanage.

"Yes. Don't you see? They want us to be invisible but we're not, not really. We're there and we can listen and see and understand. But to them, they only see us when they want to. And that, Verity, gives us a real advantage."

"I'd never thought of it like that before," Verity said slowly. "You're right, Joanie. Clever old you."

We had reached the turn in the lane by now and the manor itself was slowly revealed as we walked on further. Verity made a whistling sound with pursed lips. "Goodness, Joan, you weren't joking. It's enormous."

"It is," I agreed.

"But it's not a happy house, is it?" she said, frowning. "Not a pleasant place. Rather sinister, in fact."

"Yes, absolutely."

Far ahead of us, I could see the tiny figure of Miss Cleo crossing the lawns in front of the manor. A tennis racket swung from her hand. I swallowed.

"Steady," said Verity, who had heard the change in my breathing. "Invisible, remember?"

I threw her a grateful smile. "It's a bit of an adventure, isn't it, V?"

My heart was hammering. Verity nodded and smiled, tensely. "I'm ready, if you are."

I INTRODUCED VERITY TO THE other servants. It was my afternoon off that day and everyone thought Verity and I would do something like go out for tea and cake. If they only knew what we had planned for the afternoon... I looked out Annie's spare uniform for Verity and she wriggled into it quickly, up in my room. I helped her pin her hair back and put on the cap. She pulled on white cotton gloves.

"What if someone comes?" she hissed as we made our way to the room in question.

"You're a new member of staff, that's all," I said, more calmly than I felt. Now that we were near the lion's den, so to speak, I could feel sweat prickling on my upper lip. My hands were actually shaking.

We paused for a moment, outside the door. I took a deep breath, knocked, listened, knocked again and finally opened the door. I knew the room would be empty but it was best to be on the safe side.

"Go on," I whispered to Verity. "I'll stand guard."

She was only in there for about ten minutes, but it felt a lot longer than that. I'd brought up a duster and was industrially applying it to the skirting boards along the passageway, as I kept a sharp ear and eye out for anyone coming. Once, Violet passed me and gave me a puzzled look – I knew she was wondering why the head kitchen maid was up in the corridor, dusting the walls – but she was clearly in a hurry and so didn't stop to ask.

The door creaked behind me and I sprang up, heart fluttering. Verity emerged, neat in her uniform, her face buttoned down, expressing nothing. She was empty handed.

"You didn't—" I began. A great wave of disappointment crashed over me, followed by one of humiliation. Was I making the biggest fool of myself in this? Did I have everything wrong?

Verity didn't say anything but she gave a miniscule shake of her head. She set off up the corridor at a fast walk and I hurried after her.

Safely up in my room, the door bolted, I put my hands up to my face in despair.

"You couldn't find anything? V – I was so sure..."

"Hold your horses," said Verity. She unbuttoned the top three buttons of her dress, reached inside and drew out two things with a flourish, like a magician drawing a rabbit from a hat. I reached for them.

"Wait," she said. "Put gloves on."

"Oh, yes." I looked out my clean pair of gloves, the only spare pair I had. Once I'd slid them on, Verity put both finds into my hands: a small, hessian bag and a photograph. The photograph was blank side up. I turned it over and choked.

"I know," said Verity, taking it back from me. "Sorry, Joan. I should have warned you."

I shook my head, unable to say anything for a moment. Then, dismissing the image I'd just seen from my mind, I opened the bag. Even though I was expecting what I found inside, I still felt a coldness spread through me, as if I'd swallowed a long drink of cold water. The bag was full of small, round black seeds.

I looked up at Verity and she nodded, her face grave. "I think that's all we'll need, Joan."

"Yes," I said, looking down at our finds. "I think so, too."

I had never set foot in a police station before. Verity and I both stepped over the threshold and looked about us nervously. I think we were expecting to see ruffians being wrestled to the floor and billy clubs being whacked about while sirens went off but, in the event, the room just had a black and white checkered floor (rather dirty), the front desk behind which sat a pink-faced and cherubic looking young constable, and a couple of benches stood against the wall.

I asked to see Inspector Maxwell, in a voice that was rather more hesitant and tremulous than I would have liked it to be. Luckily, the inspector passed behind the desk as we were standing there and overheard his name. We found ourselves being ushered into a room that stood off the corridor behind the desk. It was nondescript, furnished only with a wooden table and four chairs.

"Now then," said the inspector as he showed us to our seats. "What can I do for you, ladies?"

Verity and I exchanged a glance. Now we were actually here, it sounded so ridiculous. I could feel my hands start shaking again and I clutched at my bag, remembering what I'd put inside it. That was evidence, solid evidence. The thought of it calmed me a little.

"We're here because we have some information for you, to do with the murder of Delphine Denford," said Verity, clearly realising that I'd been struck dumb.

"The *murder* of Delphine Denford," repeated the inspector. "You think she was murdered, do you?"

I tried to say something, but I couldn't get my mouth to work properly. Verity took up the reins again. "Yes," she said, sounding almost cheerful. "We know who did it, you see."

They say you can't shock a policeman. True to this saying, Inspector Maxwell merely raised his eyebrows a little. "Indeed?"

"Yes," said Verity, staring him straight in the eyes. Her chin was up a little. "She was killed by her husband."

Silence descended over the room like a grey cloak for a moment. The inspector's eyebrows rose slowly again. "Now, that is a very serious allegation," he said, quietly. "You do realise that Mr. Denford has not been charged with any sort of crime?"

Somehow, I got my voice to work. It came out a little croaky at first but soon strengthened. "Sir, I know this must seem ridiculous to you, coming from us. But you must believe us, sir, that we have good reason to believe that Mr. Denford – well, did this terrible thing."

The inspector leant back in his chair and steepled his fingers in front of his chin. "Mr. Denford was away from the manor on the night of his wife's death. He was staying at his club, in London. Many, many irreproachable witnesses place him there for the entire night. How is it possible that he caused his wife's death if he wasn't even in the house?"

"Oh, he wasn't working alone," said Verity. "His lover was the one who actually killed her."

"His lover?" The eyebrows went up again.

The room fell silent once more. I could hear the faint regular tick of the clock over on the far wall.

I could see the inspector thinking quickly. "His lover?" He repeated. "You don't mean Miss Cleo Maddox...?"

I shook my head.

The inspector's tone was scathing. "You're not telling me that you suspect Mr. Denford of having an affair with his middle-aged *aunt*?"

"Of course not, sir," said Verity. "We're talking about his lover. Mr. John Manfield."

There was another moment of silence, even longer than the first. It was broken only by the buzzing of a fly at the windowpane, a monotonous drone that seemed to fill the otherwise silent room.

The inspector was staring intently at both of us over the tops of his fingers. I think he was starting to wonder if we were both a little mad. We certainly sounded mad enough in our theories.

Before he could say anything else, I opened my bag for the evidence. "Mr. Manfield and Mr. Denford were friends out in Africa," I said hurriedly. "Mr. Manfield actually introduced Mr. Denford to his sister. "

"I know this," said the inspector, a note of disgust creeping into his voice. "So, why on Earth would you two young ladies make such sordid allegations against these two gentlemen?"

I said nothing but placed the photograph in my gloved hands on the table in front of him, face down as Verity had given it to me. He unsteepled his fingers, drew a spotless handkerchief from the breast pocket of his suit and, holding the photograph with cotton-covered fingers, turned it right side up.

They were wrong. It turns out you *can* shock a policeman. He didn't make much of a noise, just a sudden rushed intake of breath. He quickly turned the photograph face down on his desk.

"You girls should not be exposed to that sort of thing," he said sternly. "Where on Earth did you get it?"

"Mr. Manfield's room, sir," Verity's eyes had a little sparkle in them – I had the feeling she was slightly amused at the inspector's reaction. You never could shock Verity. That was what being brought up with actors led to. "He'd hidden it well – extremely well – but I knew where to look."

"You did?" asked the inspector, slightly feebly. "Why on Earth would you know?"

"I'm a housemaid, sir." The sparkle in her eyes was more apparent now. "I know everybody's secrets and where they hide them."

"Indeed." The inspector looked down at the blank back of the photograph again. "You shouldn't have touched this," he went on, his tone suddenly stern.

"We wore gloves, sir," I said quickly. "We didn't touch anything without gloves."

"Even so—"

"And there's this," I blurted out, remembering what else we had found. I gave him the little hessian bag and he took it, frowning and looked within it.

"I suppose you're going to tell me what these are?"

I looked at Verity and she nodded, taking over. She explained about the mistress's illness, her symptoms, Tenganka, the seeds of the sickness tree and how Mr. Manfield had told me about the way people were ill-wished and died. The inspector didn't say anything as she spoke, but he nodded at intervals. When she finally finished speaking, he was looking slightly winded.

A third silence fell. I was thinking hard. I had that one final bit of evidence to disclose, but to do so would mark me out as horribly immodest, even someone worse than that – a voyeur, a peeping Tom. But I had to say something, didn't I? I thought of that verse from the Bible. *And the Truth shall set you free...*

I told the inspector of how I'd crept out at night and waited in hiding outside Mr. Denford's door. I told him how I'd seen Mr. Manfield creep down the corridor like a shadow and enter Mr. Denford's room. Then, my face fiery as if I were standing in front of a furnace, I told him what I'd heard.

"That was my proof," I said, tremulously. The inspector looked as though he didn't know whether to clap me on the shoulder to congratulate me for my quick thinking or arrest me for deviance. I could feel Verity beside me give me a quick, friendly nudge with her elbow; a kind of 'I'm here for you' nudge. I straightened my back and spoke more firmly. "But you see, sir, I couldn't come to you with just that. Verity and I knew that we had to have concrete proof, either of the method of poisoning or of their – their affection."

I stopped speaking. I could hear the fly buzzing again, and saw it moving in slow, looping circles, over by the light on the wall.

"Well," said the inspector. "Seeing as you girls seem to know everything about the case, perhaps you'll tell me why you think the two men did this?"

Verity and I exchanged a glance. We knew, that

he knew, that we knew he knew full well why the murder had taken place. But – and I think we both realised this – it was his way of saying thank you. It was his tribute to our hard work.

"Money," I said. "The will benefits Mr. Denford directly. He and his – Mr. Manfield – get to share the proceeds, which wouldn't have happened if Mrs. Denford had divorced him. I think she found out about their – their affair. I came across her, just before she died, and she'd had a dreadful shock. I think she'd found out about them. She said 'I don't know what to do' and, very soon after that, she died. I think they couldn't risk her talking or making any kind of scandal. So to be sure of the money, they had to kill her."

"Money," said the inspector. "That's at the root of most crimes, it's true."

"And love," Verity said suddenly. The inspector and I both looked at her. "They did it for love."

I said nothing. The inspector shook his head a little, as if to clear her words from his ears. That look of disgust was back on his face.

"Yes," I said, considering. "Perhaps for love, too."

WE WERE OFFERED A LIFT back from the station but refused it. Verity had to catch a train back to London and I wanted to see her off. We had to wait on the platform for a bit and found a bench to sit on. I felt strangely flat after all the excitement, as if the curtain had come down on a rather unsatisfying play.

"Why don't you come back to London with me, Joanie?" Verity asked impulsively.

I hesitated. I wanted to, so much, despite not having any of my possessions with me. Just jump on a train back to the Smoke and hang the consequences. But no – after a sudden blazing desire to do just that, reality intruded and I shook my head regretfully.

"I can't, V. I've got to work my notice out, you know that. I won't get a decent reference otherwise and without that, how can I work?"

"Yes, I know," said Verity with a sigh. "So you're definitely going to hand in your notice?"

"Yes. I've had enough of this place. It's time to come back to London."

"Well, that *is* good news." Her train had puffed into the station, steaming like a kettle. I helped her into her third class compartment and she slid the window in the door down and reached her hand out to me. "Good work, Joanie. Don't you think? Wasn't it exciting?"

I laughed. "It certainly was. Better than cooking, that's for sure!"

We clasped hands and then, as the train hooted, let go. I watched her move away from me as the train left the platform, her frantically waving hand the last thing I could see before the clouds of steam and smoke swallowed her up. My own hand dropped back to my side.

I walked back to the manor. I had lost all track of time but the sun was low in the sky, shining on the windows of the huge house as I rounded the corner of the footpath, so that they glittered and shone as if a fire burned behind the thousands of panes of glass. I was fifty yards away when I saw the cars come down the driveway, three of them. I stopped dead, level with the edge of the lawns. From my vantage point. I could see the inspector and three uniformed officers walk up the long sweep of steps to the front door. They weren't hurrying but they had a grim, unrelenting rhythm to their stride that made me realise that they weren't going to leave unaccompanied.

I stayed where I was for five long minutes, my hand clutching at the rough bark of the tree next to me. I could hear my heart thrumming, a thunder of blood in my ears. When the policeman reappeared, they had both Mr. Denford and Mr. Manfield with them. Both had their hands cuffed in front of them. Miss Cleo stood to one side, clasping her arms across her body. I thought of how she'd always seemed to dislike Mr. Manfield. Could she have known what he was, and what he was doing to his sister? Surely not the latter, or wouldn't she have said something? Perhaps she'd known, or sensed what he really was.

The two men were taken to the vehicles. I was too far away to see properly but it looked as though they reached out to one another, before they were roughly dragged away and put in separate cars. Absurd tears sprang to my eyes. I scrubbed them away with my sleeve, looking up and away, my gaze resting on the pine forest behind the house. From this viewpoint, it encircled the manor like the black, shaggy paws of a giant beast. I thought of Mr. Manfield, of meeting him in the forest and how he'd always been kind to me. But he was a murderer, who'd cold-bloodedly poisoned his own sister, giving her the sickness seeds in his own mug of hot milk. He was the one who'd washed the cups and hung them back up; I realised that now. That would be something else to tell the inspector. I remembered what he'd said in the woods. *Human sacrifice*. Had that given him and the master the idea? Was it Astarte, working through them, wanting her pound of flesh, wanting their souls? *Are you satisfied now*? I asked her silently and then I shivered, because a small, superstitious part of me knew that you didn't rouse the attention of the goddess. Not if you knew what was good for you.

I would write about this, one day, I realised. I thought of the silly play Verity and I had seen, *Death at the Manor*, and thought, no, I will write the *real* play, the one it should have been. I knew I could do it. I had it in me.

The sun had disappeared behind grey clouds and it was beginning to rain. I tore my eyes from Astarte's forest and began to walk back to the manor, for the last time.

THE END

Enjoyed this book? An honest review left at Amazon, Goodreads, Shelfari and LibraryThing is always welcome and *really* important for indie authors. The more reviews an independently published book has, the easier it is to market it and find new readers.

Want some more of Celina Grace's work for free? Subscribers to her mailing list get a free digital copy of **Requiem (A Kate Redman Mystery: Book 2)**, a free digital copy of **A Prescription for Death (The Asharton Manor Mysteries Book 2)** *and* a free PDF copy of her short story collection **A Blessing From The Obeah Man.**

Requiem (A Kate Redman Mystery: Book 2)

WHEN THE BODY OF TROUBLED teenager Elodie Duncan is pulled from the river in Abbeyford, the case is at first assumed to be a straightforward suicide. Detective Sergeant Kate Redman is shocked to discover that she'd met the victim the night before her death, introduced by Kate's younger brother Jay. As the case develops, it becomes clear that Elodie was murdered. A talented young musician, Elodie had been keeping some strange company and was hiding her own dark secrets.

As the list of suspects begin to grow, so do the questions. What is the significance of the painting Elodie modelled for? Who is the man who was seen with her on the night of her death? Is there any connection with another student's death at the exclusive musical college that Elodie attended?

As Kate and her partner Detective Sergeant Mark Olbeck attempt to unravel the mystery, the dark undercurrents of the case threaten those whom Kate holds most dear...

A Prescription for Death (The Asharton Manor Mysteries: Book 2) – a novella

"I HAD A SURGE OF kinship the first time I saw the manor, perhaps because we'd both seen better days."

It is 1947. Asharton Manor, once one of the most beautiful stately homes in the West Country, is now a convalescent home for former soldiers. Escaping the devastation of post-war London is Vivian Holt, who moves to the nearby village and begins to volunteer as a nurse's aide at the manor. Mourning the death of her soldier husband, Vivian finds solace in her new friendship with one of the older patients, Norman Winter, someone who has served his country in both world wars. Slowly, Vivian's heart begins to heal, only to be torn apart when she arrives for work one day to be told that Norman is dead.

It seems a straightforward death, but is it? Why did a particular photograph disappear from Norman's possessions after his death? Who is the sinister figure who keeps following Vivian? Suspicion and doubts begin to grow and when another death occurs, Vivian begins to realise that the war may be over but the real battle is just beginning...

A Blessing From The Obeah Man

DARE YOU READ ON? HORRIFYING, scary, sad and thought-provoking, this short story collection will take you on a macabre journey. In the titular story, a honeymooning couple take a wrong turn on their trip around Barbados. The Mourning After brings you a shiversome story from a suicidal teenager. In Freedom Fighter, an unhappy middle-aged man chooses the wrong day to make a bid for freedom, whereas Little Drops of Happiness and Wave Goodbye are tales of darkness from sunny Down Under. Strapping Lass and The Club are for those who prefer, shall we say, a little meat to the story...

JUST GO TO CELINA'S BLOG on writing and self-publishing to sign up. It's quick, easy and free. Be the first to be informed of promotions, giveaways, new releases and subscriber-only benefits by subscribing to her (occasional) newsletter.

http://www.celinagrace.com
Twitter: @celina__grace
Facebook: http://www.facebook.com/authorcelinagrace

Miss Hart and Miss Hunter Investigate...

"A GOOD SERVANT HAS TO be invisible. So does a good detective."

Joan and Verity return in 2015 for their own series of historical mysteries, set in the 1920s and 30s. Sign up to Celina's mailing list on her website http://www.celinagrace.com to be kept informed on how the series is progressing, publication dates and other writing news...

Miss Hart and Miss Hunter Investigate...

The new series starring Joan Hart and Verity Hunter

Coming to Amazon in 2015

A Prescription for Death is the second in The Asharton Manor Mysteries series.

Please note - this is a novella-length piece of fiction (about 20 thousand words)

"I HAD A SURGE OF kinship the first time I saw the manor, perhaps because we'd both seen better days."

It is 1947. Asharton Manor, once one of the most beautiful stately homes in the West Country, is now a convalescent home for former soldiers. Escaping the devastation of post-war London is Vivian Holt, who moves to the nearby village and begins to volunteer as a nurse's aide at the manor. Mourning the death of her soldier husband, Vivian finds solace in her new friendship with one of the older patients, Norman Winter, someone who has served his country in both world wars. Slowly, Vivian's heart begins to heal, only to be torn apart when she arrives for work one day to be told that Norman is dead.

It seems a straightforward death, but is it? Why did a particular photograph disappear from Norman's possessions after his death? Who is the sinister figure who keeps following Vivian?

Suspicion and doubts begin to grow and when another death occurs, Vivian begins to realise that the war may be over but the real battle is just beginning...

Buy **A Prescription for Death,**
available from Amazon now.

The Rhythm of Murder is
the third in The Asharton
Manor Mysteries series.

IT IS 1973. EVE AND Janey, two young university
students, are en route to a Bristol commune when
they take an unexpected detour to the little village
of Midford. Seduced by the roguish charms of a
young man who picks them up in the village pub,
they are astonished to find themselves at Asharton
Manor, now the residence of the very wealthy, very
famous, very degenerate Blue Turner, lead singer
of rock band Dirty Rumours. The golden summer
rolls on, full of sex, drugs and rock and roll, but Eve
begins to sense that there may be a sinister side to
all the hedonism.

And then one day, Janey disappears, seemingly
run away... but as Eve begins to question what
happened to her friend, she realises that she herself
might be in terrible danger...

Buy **The Rhythm of Murder** on
Amazon, available now.

Have you met Detective Sergeant Kate Redman?

THE KATE REDMAN MYSTERIES ARE the bestselling detective mysteries from Celina Grace, featuring the flawed but determined female officer Kate Redman and her pursuit of justice in the West Country town of Abbeyford.

Hushabye (A Kate Redman Mystery: Book 1) is the novel that introduces Detective Sergeant Kate Redman on her first case in Abbeyford. It's available for free! Turn the page to read the first two chapters.

HUSHABYE

(A KATE REDMAN MYSTERY)

Celina Grace

© Celina Grace 2013

Prologue

CASEY FULLMAN OPENED HER EYES and knew something was wrong.

It was too bright. She was used to waking to grey dimness, the before-sunrise hours of a winter morning. Dita would stand by the bed with Charlie in one arm, a warmed bottle in the other. Casey would struggle up to a sitting position, trying to avoid the jab of pain from her healing Caesarean scar, and take the baby and the bottle.

You're mad to get up so early when you don't have to, her mother had told her, more than once. *It's not like you're breastfeeding. Let Dita do it*. But Casey, smiling and shrugging, would never give up those first waking moments. She enjoyed the delicious warmth of the baby snuggled against her body, his dark eyes fixed upon hers as he sucked furiously at the bottle.

She didn't envy Dita, though, stumbling back to bed through the early morning dark to her bedroom next to the nursery. Casey would have gotten up herself to take Charlie from his cot when he cried for his food, but Nick needed his sleep, and it seemed to work out better all round for Dita, so close to the cot anyway, to bring him and the bottle into the bedroom instead. That's what I pay her for, Nick had said, when she'd suggested getting up herself.

But this morning there was no Dita, sleepy-eyed in rumpled pyjamas, standing by the bed. There was no Charlie. Casey sat up sharply, wincing as her stomach muscles pulled at the scar. She looked over at Nick, fast asleep next to her. Sleeping like a baby. But where was her baby, her Charlie?

She got up and padded across the soft, expensive, sound-muffling carpet, not bothering with her dressing gown, too anxious now to delay. It was almost full daylight; she could see clearly. The bedroom door was shut, and she opened it to a silent corridor outside.

The door to Dita's room was standing open, but the door to Charlie's nursery was closed. Casey looked in Dita's room. Her nanny's bed was empty, the room in its usual mess, clothes and toys all over the floor. She must have gone into Charlie's room. They must both be in there. Why hadn't Dita brought him through? He must be ill, thought Casey, and fear broke over her like a wave. Her palm slipped on the door handle to the nursery.

She pushed the door. It stuck, halfway open. Casey shoved harder and it moved, opening wide enough for her to see an out-flung arm on the carpet, a hand half-curled. Her throat closed up. Frantically, she pushed at the door, and it opened far enough to enable her to squeeze inside.

It was Dita she saw first, spread-eagled on the floor, face upwards. For a split second, Casey thought, crazily, that it was a model of her nanny, a waxwork, something that someone had left in the room for a joke. Dita's face was pale as colourless candle wax, but that wasn't the worst thing. There was something wrong with the structure of her face, her forehead dented, her nose pushed to one side. Her thick blonde hair was fanned out around her head like the stringy petals of a giant flower.

Casey felt her heartbeat falter as she looked down at the body. She was dimly aware that her lungs felt as if they'd seized up, frozen solid. She mouthed like a fish, gasping for air, but it wasn't until she moved her gaze from Dita to look at Charlie's cot that she began to scream.

Chapter One

KATE REDMAN STOOD IN THE tiny hallway of her flat and regarded herself in the full-length mirror that hung beside the front door. She never left the flat without giving herself a quick once-over—not for reasons of vanity, but to check that all was in place. She smoothed down her hair and tugged at her jacket, pulling the shoulders more firmly into shape. Her bag stood by the front door mat. She picked it up and checked her purse and mobile and warrant card were all there, zipped away in the inner pocket.

She was early, but then she was always early. Time for a quick coffee before the doorbell was expected to ring? She walked into the small, neat kitchen, her hand hovering over the kettle. She decided against it. She felt jittery enough already. *Calm down, Kate.*

It was awful being the new girl; it was like being back at school again. Although now at least, she was well-dressed, with clean hair and clean shoes.

It was fairly unlikely that any of her new co-workers would tell her that she smelt and had nits.

Kate shook herself mentally. She was talking to herself again, the usual internal monologue, always a sign of stress. It's just a new job. You can do it. They picked you, remember?

She checked her watch. He was late, although not by much. The traffic at this time of day was always awful. She walked from the kitchen to the lounge – living room, Kate, living room – a matter of ten steps. She closed her bedroom door, and then opened it again to let the air flow in. She walked back to the hallway just as the doorbell finally rang. She took a deep breath and fixed her smile in place before she opened it.

"DS Redman?" asked the man on the doorstep. "I'm DS Olbeck. Otherwise known as Mark. Bloody awful parking around here. Sorry I'm late."

Kate noted a few things immediately: the fact that he'd said 'bloody,' whereas every other copper she'd ever known would have said 'fucking'; his slightly too long dark hair; that he had a nice, crinkle-eyed smile. She felt a bit better.

"No drama," she said breezily. "I'm ready. Call me Kate."

When they got to the car, she hesitated slightly for a moment, unsure of whether she should clear the passenger seat of all the assorted crap that was piled upon it or whether she should leave it to Mark.

He muttered an apology and threw everything into the back.

"I'm actually quite neat," he said, swinging the door open for her, "but it doesn't seem to extend to the car, if you see what I mean."

Kate smiled politely. As he swung the car out into the road, she fixed her mind on the job ahead of them.

"Can you tell me–" she began, just as he began to ask her a question.

"You're from–"

"Oh, sorry–"

"I was going to say, you're up from Bournemouth, aren't you?" Olbeck asked.

"That's right. I grew up there."

"I thought that's where people went to retire."

Kate grinned. "Pretty much. There's wasn't a lot of, shall we say, life when I was growing up." She paused. "Still, we had the beach. Where are you from?"

"London," said DS Olbeck, briefly. There was a pause while he waited to join the dual carriageway. "Nowhere glamorous. Just the outskirts, really. Ruislip, Middlesex. How are you finding the move to the West Country?"

"Fine so far."

"Have you got family around here?

Kate was growing impatient with the small talk.

"No, no one around here," she said. "Can I ask you about the case?"

"Of course."

"I know it's a murder and kidnap case—"

"Yes. The child – baby – belongs to the Fullmans. Nick Fullman is a very wealthy entrepreneur, made most of his cash in property development. He got married about a year ago – to one of those sort of famous people."

"How do you mean?" Kate asked.

"Oh you know, the sort of Z-list celebrity that keeps showing up in Heat magazine. Her name's Casey Bright. Well, Casey Fullman now. Appeared in Okay when they got married, showing you round their lovely home, you know the sort of thing."

Kate smiled. "I get the picture."

She wouldn't have pegged DS Olbeck for a gossip mag reader, but then people often weren't what they seemed.

"And the murder?"

"The nanny, Dita Olgweisch. Looks incidental to the kidnapping at this point, but you never know. What is known is that the baby is missing and as it – he's – only three months old, you can imagine the kind of thing we're dealing with here."

"Yes." Kate was silent for a moment. A three-month-old baby...memories threatened to surface and she pushed them away. "So on the face of it, we're looking at the baby was snatched, the nanny interrupted whoever it was, and she was killed?"

"Like you say, on the surface, that seems to be what's happened. We'll know more soon. We'll be there in," he glanced at the sat nav on the windscreen, "fifteen minutes or so."

They were off the motorway now and into the countryside. Looking out of the window, Kate noted the ploughed fields, shorn of the autumn stubble, the skeletal shapes of the trees. It was a grey January day, the sky like a flat blanket the colour of nothing. The worst time of year, she thought, everything dead, shut down for the winter, months until spring.

The car slowed, turned into a driveway, and continued through formidable iron gates which were opened for them by a uniformed officer. After they drove through, Kate looked back to see the gates swung shut behind them. She noted the high wooden fence that ran alongside the road, the CCTV camera on the gatepost. The driveway wound through dripping trees and opened out into a courtyard at the front of the house.

"Looks like security is a priority," she said to her companion as he pulled the car up by the front door.

He raised his eyebrows. "Clearly not enough of a priority."

"Well, we'll see," said Kate.

They both got out of the car. There was another

uniformed officer by the front door, a pale redhead whose nose had reddened in the raw air. He was stamping his feet and swinging his arms but stopped abruptly when Kate and Olbeck reached him.

"DCI Anderton here yet?" said Olbeck.

"Yes sir. He's inside, in the kitchen. Just go straight through the hallway."

They stepped inside. The hallway was cavernous, tiled in chilly white stone, scuffed and marked now with the imprint of shoes and boots. Kate looked around. A staircase split in two and flowed around the upper reaches of the hallway to the first floor of the house. There was an enormous light shade suspended from the ceiling, a tangled mass of glass tubing and metal filaments. It had probably cost more than her flat, but she thought it hideous all the same. The house was warm, too warm; the underfloor heating was obviously at full blast, but there was an atmosphere of frigidity nonetheless. Perhaps it was the glossy white floor, the high ceilings, the general air of too much space. A Philip Starke chair stood against the wall, looking as though it had been carved out of ice.

"Mark? That you? Through here."

They followed the shout through into the kitchen, big on an industrial scale. It opened out into a glass-walled conservatory, which overlooked a terrace leading down to a clipped and manicured lawn. Detective Chief Inspector Anderton stood by a cluster of leather sofas where a woman was sitting, crouching forward, her long blonde hair dipping towards the floor. Kate looked around her surreptitiously. The place stank of money, new money: wealth just about dripped from the ceilings. It must be a kidnapping. Now, Kate, she chided herself. No jumping to conclusions.

She had only met the Chief Inspector once before, at her interview. He was a grey man: steel grey hair, dark grey eyes, grey suit. Easy to dismiss, at first.

"Ah, DS Redman," he said as they both approached. "Welcome. Hoping to catch up with you later in my office, but we'll have to see how things go. You can see how things are here."

He gave her a firm handshake, holding her gaze for a moment. She was surprised at the sudden tug of her lower belly, a pulse that vanished almost as soon as she'd registered it. A little shaken, it took her a moment to collect herself. The other two officers had begun talking to the blonde woman on the sofa. Kate joined them.

Casey Fullman was a tiny woman, very childlike in spite of the bleached hair, the breast implants and the false nails. Kate noted the delicate bones of her wrist and ankles. Casey had bunchy cheeks, smooth and round like the curve of a peach, a tip-tilted nose and large blue eyes. These last were bloodshot, tears glistening along the edge of her reddened eyelids.

"I don't know," she was saying as Kate joined them. Her voice was high, and she spoke with a gasp that could have been tears but might be habitual. "I don't know. I didn't hear anything and when I woke up, Dita," she drew in her breath, "Dita wasn't there. She would normally be there with a bottle and Ch– and Ch–"

She broke down entirely, dropping her head down to her bare knees. There was a moment of silence while Kate watched the ends of Casey's long hair touch the floor.

Anderton began to utter some soothing words. Kate looked around, her eye attracted by a movement outside on the terrace. A man was walking up and down, talking into a mobile phone, his free hand gesticulating wildly. As Kate watched, he flipped the phone closed and turned towards the house. He was young, good-looking and, somewhat incongruously given the early hour, dressed in a suit.

"Sorry about that, I had to take it," said Nick Fullman as he entered the room. Kate mentally raised her eyebrows, wondering at a man who prioritised a phone call, presumably a business matter, over comforting his wife after their baby son had been kidnapped. Not necessarily a kidnapping, Kate, stop jumping to conclusions. She thought she saw an answering disapproval in Olbeck's face.

Anderton introduced his colleagues. Nick Fullman shook hands with them both, rather to Kate's surprise, and then finally sat down next to his sobbing wife.

"Come on, Case," he said, pulling her up and encircling her with one arm. "Try and keep it together. The police are here to help."

Casey put shaking fingers up to her mouth. She appeared to be trying to control her tears, taking in deep, shuddering breaths.

"Perhaps you'd like a cup of tea?" said Olbeck. He caught Kate's eye, and she immediately looked away. *Don't you bloody dare ask me to make it.* He looked around rather helplessly. "Is there anyone who could , er–"

"I'll make it."

They all looked around at the sound of the words. A woman had come into the kitchen. Or had she? Kate wondered whether she'd been there all along, unnoticed. There was something unmemorable about her, which was odd because she too was dressed in full business attire, her face heavily made-up, her hair straightened and twisted and pinned in an elaborate style on the top of her head.

"This is my PA, Gemma Phillips," said Fullman. There was just a shade of relief in his voice. "Gemma, thanks for coming so quickly."

"It's fine," she said with a brilliant smile, a smile

that faded a little as she surveyed Casey, huddled and gasping. "It's terrible. I came as quickly as I could. I can't believe it."

"If you could make tea for us all, that would be wonderful, Miss Phillips," said Anderton.

"It's Ms Phillips, if you don't mind," she said, rather quickly. "Or you can call me Gemma. I don't mind."

Anderton inclined his head.

"Of course. We'd like to talk to you as well, once we've been able to sit with Mr and Mrs Fullman for a while."

He turned back to the Fullmans. Gemma shrugged and began to make tea, moving quickly about the room. Kate watched her. Clearly Gemma knew her way around the kitchen very well. What, exactly, was her relationship with her employers like? Had she worked for them long? Presumably she didn't live on the premises. Kate made mental notes to use in her interview with the girl later.

The tea was made and presented to them all. Casey took one sip of hers and choked.

"Oh, sorry," said Gemma. "I always forget you don't take sugar."

There was something in her voice that made Kate's internal sensor light up. Not mockery, not exactly. There was something though. Kate scribbled more mental notes.

Nick Fullman had been given coffee, rather than

tea, in an elegant white china cup. He'd swallowed it in three gulps. Kate noted the dark shadows under his eyes and the faint jittery shudder of his fingers. A caffeine addict? An insomniac? Or something else?

"I heard nothing," he was saying in response to Anderton's question. "I was sleeping. I sleep pretty heavily, and the first I knew about anything was Casey screaming down the hallway. I ran down and saw, well, saw Dita on the floor. "

"Do you have any theories as to who might have taken your son?"

Casey let out a small moan. Nick pulled her closer to him.

"None whatsoever. I can't believe anyone-" His voice faltered for a second. "I can't believe anyone would do such a thing."

"No one has made any threats against you or your family recently?"

"Of course not."

"Who has access to the house? Do you keep any staff?"

Fullman frowned. "What do you mean by access?"

"Well, keys specifically. But also anyone who is permitted to enter the house, particularly on a regular basis."

"I'll have to think." Fullman was silent for a moment. He looked at his personal assistant.

"Gemma, you couldn't be a star and make another coffee, could you?"

"Of course." Gemma almost jumped from her chair to fulfil his request.

Fullman turned back to the police officers.

"Casey and I have keys, of course. Gemma has a set to the house, although not to the outbuildings, I don't think."

"That's right," called Gemma from the kitchen. "Just the house."

"What about Miss Olgweisch?"

Fullman dropped his eyes to the floor. "Yes, Dita had a full set."

"Anyone else?"

Casey raised her head from her husband's shoulder.

"My mum's got a front door key," she said, her voice hoarse. "She knows the key codes and all that."

"Ah, yes," said Anderton. "The security. Presumably all the people who have keys also have security codes and so forth?"

Fullman nodded. "That's right. There's an access code on the main gate and the alarm code for the house."

Kate and Olbeck exchanged glances. Whoever had taken the baby hadn't set off any of the alarms.

Casey pushed herself upright.

"What are you doing to find him?" she begged.

"Why are we sat here answering all these questions when we should be out there looking for him?"

"Mrs Fullman," said Anderton in a steady tone. "I really do know how desperate you must be feeling. My officers are out there on your land combing every inch of it for clues to Charlie's whereabouts. We just have to try and ascertain a few basic facts so we can think of the best way to move forward as quickly as possible."

"It's just..." Casey's voice trailed away. Kate addressed her husband.

"Mr Fullman, is there anyone who could come and give your wife some support? Give you both some support? Her mother, perhaps?"

Fullman grimaced. "I suppose so. Case, shall I ring your mum?" His wife nodded, mutely, and he stood up. "I'll go and ring her then."

He headed back outside to the terrace, clearly relieved to be escaping the kitchen. Olbeck looked at Kate and raised his eyebrows very slightly. She nodded, just as subtly.

"You two look around," said Anderton. "DS Redman, I'd like you to talk to Ms Phillips once you're done. DS Olbeck, go and see how the search is progressing. I want the neighbours questioned before too long."

The house was newly built, probably less than ten years old. It was a sprawling low building, cedar-clad and white-rendered, technically built on several different levels but as the ground had been dug away and landscaped around it, the house looked like nothing so much as a very expensive bungalow. Or so Kate thought, walking around the perimeter with Olbeck. They had checked the layout of the bedrooms, noting the distance of the baby's nursery from the Fullman's bedroom.

"Why wasn't the baby in their room?" asked Kate.

Olbeck glanced at her. "Should he have been?"

"I think that's the standard advice. Everyone I know with tiny babies keeps them in their own bedrooms. Sometimes in their beds. Not stuck down the end of the corridor."

"I don't know," said Olbeck. "The nanny was right next door."

Dita Olgweisch's room and the nursery were still sealed off by the Scene of Crime team gathering evidence. Kate stood back for a second to let a SOCO past her, rustling along in white overalls.

"I'll ask Mrs Fullman when she's feeling up to it," she said. "Perhaps there was a simple explanation."

The view from the terrace was undeniably lovely. The ground dropped steeply away from the decking and the lawn ended in a semi-circle of woodland; beech, ash, and oak trees all stood as if on guard around the grass. Kate could see the movements of the uniformed officers as they carried out their fingertip search. Olbeck came up beside her and they both stood looking out on the scene. Kate wondered if he was thinking what she was thinking – that somewhere out in those peaceful looking woods was a tiny child's body. Her stomach clenched.

"I've never worked on a child case before," said Olbeck abruptly. Kate turned her head, surprised. "Murder, obviously. But never a child."

"We don't know that the baby's..." Kate didn't want to finish the sentence.

"I know." They were both silent for a moment. "I hope you're right. God, I hope you're right."

There didn't seem to be much else to say. They both had things to do, but for another moment, they stood quietly, side by side, looking out at the swaying, leafless branches of the trees.

***

ACKNOWLEDGEMENTS

MANY THANKS TO ALL THE following splendid souls:

Chris Howard for the brilliant cover designs; Andrea Harding for editing and proofreading; Kathy McConnell for extra proofreading and beta reading; lifelong Schlockers and friends David Hall, Ben Robinson and Alberto Lopez; Ross McConnell for advice on police procedural and for also being a great brother; Kathleen and Pat McConnell, Anthony Alcock, Naomi White, Mo Argyle, Lee Benjamin, Bonnie Wede, Sherry and Amali Stoute, Cheryl Lucas, Georgia Lucas-Going, Steven Lucas, Loletha Stoute and Harry Lucas, Helen Parfect, Helen Watson, Emily Way, Sandy Hall, Kristýna Vosecká; and of course my patient and ever-loving Chris, Mabel, Jethro and Isaiah.

Printed in Great Britain
by Amazon

37505031R00073